For Ma[...]

You're as mad as me
Love Pete Donohue

STORIES FOR THE xy MAD

VOLUME ONE

MORAN PRESS

ISBN: 978-0-9979491-9-3

Moran Press

Blackstone, MA

INTRODUCTION

"Literature is a quilt, squares collected over the ages, roughly stitched and assembled in the dark. May each writer join with voices gathered together in time, take your place in the grand story." Edgardo Vega Yunqué - - May 20, 1936 - August 26, 2008

"Follow your most intense obsessions mercilessly." Franz Kafka

My writing mentor, Edgardo Vegas Yunqué, described literature as a conversation between writers throughout the ages, what you write and publish melds and becomes one with the story set down before you.

Two of my great loves in all literature are Edgar Allan Poe and Franz Kafka. Both inspired me to read and ultimately to write short fiction. I want *Stories for the Mad* to continue the conversation their stories began of characters trying to navigate a nightmarish world filled with absurdity and dread.

To achieve this end, I read the submissions for this anthology between readings of Kafka and Poe. I'd read a submission, followed by a story. I added Poe and Kafka stories to the manuscript I was assembling of my favorite submissions.

I read and re-read the manuscript, adding submissions and removing those that didn't quite fit in the mix. I read it several times until I arrived at the final roster of stories. Included in this volume are one story each from Poe and Kafka I believe are suited to this collection. Without further delay, I present:

Stories for the Mad. The debut short fiction anthology from Moran Press.

STORIES FOR THE MAD

BONUS CONTENT

LOVE AND ROCKETS
Rae Theodore

The first time I proposed to Daphne, I paid a guy to fly a banner over the beach.

It was the 4th of July weekend, and Daphne and I were staying at the Jersey shore.

On Saturday, Daphne wanted to go into town and shop.

"Darling, please, let's go to the beach," I had begged. "I'll buy you whatever you want tomorrow."

She had agreed but spent most of the time lying on her stomach with her eyes closed.

I stared at my watch and the cornflower blue sky, waiting to catch a glimpse of the little prop plane pulling a bright white banner with the words "MARRY ME" in capital letters.

When I saw it, I nudged Daphne.

"What?" she said.

"Sweetums, I have something I want you to see."

"I agreed to come to the beach, Jake. Not to see what *you* want me to see," she said. "You're such a male chauvinist pig."

Daphne adjusted her position on her pink and purple striped beach towel. Her long blonde hair fanned out over her shoulders like a silky cape.

I poked her again.

"I promise you'll like it," I said.

"Fine, Jake, fine! It's always about you, isn't it?"

She sat up and stared at the ocean. "Okay, what's so important? Oh, look, water. It's blue."

She started to lay back down, but I placed my hand under her chin and gently tilted her head up toward the sky. As I looked into her soft blue eyes, I could feel my heart start to speed up.

"Will you, Daphne? Will you make me the happiest man on the planet?"

"You have got to be kidding, Jake. How do I even know that's for me? Marry me? So generic. That could be for anyone."

She jabbed her finger into the air and started pointing at random strangers.

"Really, glomming off somebody else's proposal? I thought you were better than that."

"But baby cakes ..."

Daphne stood up. Her long bronze legs seemed to stretch all the way to the clouds like the woman in the poster for the movie *Attack of the 40 Foot Woman*. She shook the sand from her towel, and the sharp spray stung my eyes.

The people around us covered their faces with their hands.

"Jesus Christ, lady," said a middle-aged man in a bright yellow Speedo. "Ain't you ever heard of beach etiquette?"

Daphne snapped her towel in his direction, slipped into her flip-flops and started walking toward the dunes and the little wooden path that led to our weekend bungalow.

"Wait!" I yelled.

She turned around and looked at me.

"I don't know what you want!" I said.

"Love and rockets! I want love and rockets!"

I tossed on my Star Wars T-shirt and started fast walking toward her on the hot sand.

"What does that mean?" I asked.

"I'll know when I see it," she said.

I watched Daphne's orange bikini bottom fade into the distance like a setting sun. She kicked up small spurts of sand as she walked as if she were her own storm. Tropical Storm Daphne.

And there I was, eight or nine years old again, watching my mom leave the house for a day or two or maybe more. Even though I knew it was coming, the slam of the screen door was a slap to my face. I always stood with the tip of my nose pressed into the mesh screen, watching her high heels set off little puffs of smoke as they crunched on the white stones that covered the crooked driveway and carried her to her red Mustang.

"Look what you've made me do," she would yell out the car window to my dad as he stood in the driveway begging her not to leave.

A few weeks later, I ran into the guy I had hired to fly the prop plane.

I was sitting at Jack's Tavern sipping a beer.

The pilot clapped me on the back and sat down next to me. "Congrats, Jake. Whatcha drinking? Let me buy you one."

"That's alright," I said.

"C'mon, you're gonna be a married man soon. Let me treat you to a cold one. Least I can do."

When I told him Daphne had said no, he apologized as if he had done something wrong.

"So sorry," he kept repeating. "That's never happened to me before."

We stayed at the bar until midnight, both of us mourning my failed marriage proposal.

"Can I ask you a question?" I said at the end of the night.

"Sure, Jake. Anything."

"Why do they call them prop planes?"

"It has to do with the engine, Jake. Prop is short for turboprop engine or turbo propeller engine. A prop plane uses a propeller for thrust," he explained.

"Oh. I thought it was because they were fake."

I started giggling.

"Like a prop in a play or a movie. I thought you were flying a pretend plane."

In my head, I pictured a toy airplane with plastic seats and a plastic pilot with a painted-on navy blue uniform.

I couldn't stop laughing.

The pilot squeezed my shoulder.

"Take care, pal," he said in a soft voice. "Take care of yourself."

That night, I dreamt about the prop plane. I heard the thwick, thwick, thwick the propeller made as it got started and then the steady hum.

In my dream, the pilot performed tricks like loops and corkscrews. The plane flew sideways and upside down. No matter the movement, the white "MARRY ME" banner trailed behind like a stray piece of toilet paper stuck to the bottom of a shoe.

And then the plane exploded in the sky and crashed to the ground. I walked along the charred debris. I found the pilot's arm severed at the elbow. I picked it up but couldn't tell if it was flesh and bone or a toy arm broken off at the plastic elbow joint.

While I tried to solve the riddle of love and rockets, Daphne and I continued to see each other. Five days a week, I picked her up from her job at the mall where she worked as an assistant to the assistant manager at Forever 21. I took Daphne out to dinner, the movies, on shopping trips.

In January, I decided to give the proposal another go.

On a Wednesday night, I dropped Daphne off at her house after her shift at Forever 21 and parked my car on a side street near her backyard.

"Love and rockets, love and rockets," I kept repeating.

I had purchased 75 triple screamer rockets from a fireworks site on the Internet, and I arranged them in the shape of a heart in the small yard.

At five minutes before midnight, I texted Daphne.

Come to the backyard for love and rockets XOXO

I waited until I saw her face in the square window in the back of the house and then got down on one knee.

Daphne opened the back door and walked down the concrete stairs and onto the patio. She crossed her arms. She was wearing a short pink cotton robe with Forever 21 light gray stretch knit ankle leggings. Her hair was wild like snakes and there in the moonlight she looked like a golden goddess who could coax an army of men to jump one by one from a skyscraper with a simple nod of her head.

"What the hell, Jake? You know I need my beauty sleep."

"Will you marry me, Daphne?"

I stood up and started lighting the rockets with a BBQ lighter. Their fuses turned red orange like the tip of a freshly lit cigarette, and they hissed for a few seconds and then shrieked like a tea kettle as they flew into the night sky in a bright white stream.

Before Daphne could answer, one of the triple screamer rockets, a dud that had been burning longer than the rest, launched itself sideways into a red metal can marked "fuel" sitting on the patio near Daphne's feet.

It started with a small spark at the bottom of her leggings. At first, the bright orange flicker seemed innocuous like a half smile or a wink. Then the growing flame climbed up the belt that hung from her robe.

Daphne started slapping her body to put out the fire. When she saw that technique wasn't working, she thrust out both arms. The sleeves of her robe caught fire and Daphne's hands burst into flames like a magic trick worthy of a show on the Las Vegas strip. She shook her hands in the chilly night air.

"Flaming jazz hands," I whispered.

Daphne never stopped amazing me.

Daphne's flawless alabaster skin melted and dripped down like candle wax, forming a final frown. Her head lit up red, orange, yellow.

I couldn't move, and I couldn't look away. The more I stared at Daphne, the more colors I saw. Blue, green, turquoise, purple.

Daphne had never looked more beautiful. She was all the colors of a Roman candle.

I wanted to hold her in my arms; it would have been like holding a piece of a rainbow. But then I've always been a romantic at heart.

I heard a whistling noise. I wasn't sure if it was coming from Daphne or the triple screamer rockets.

My face was flushed, my heart was racing like a Ferrari engine. I felt dizzy and lightheaded in a good way, as if I were a bright red helium balloon shiny with hope.

I finally understood what Daphne had wanted.

"Love and rockets," I said out loud as I walked to my car.

Rae Theodore is the author of My Mother Says Drums Are For Boys: True Stories for Gender Rebels and Leaving Normal: Adventures in Gender. Her stories and poems have appeared in numerous publications, including *Our Happy Hours: LGBT Voices from the Gay Bars, Sister Wisdom* and *Nonbinary: Memoirs of Gender.* You can read about her adventures in gender nonconformity on her blog, *The Flannel Files.* Rae is the past president of the Greater Philadelphia Chapter of the Women's National Book Association and lives in Royersford, Pennsylvania with her wife, kids, and cats. She is working on a book about love.

HITTING THE BRICKS
Scott Wozniak

As Breezy walked through the sixteen-foot-tall, mechanical, iron gates, he felt the weight of steel bars, razor wire, and one-hundred and twenty-year-old bricks fall from his shoulders. In his stomach churned a mix of anxiety, excitement, fear, and elation.

He was finally boarding the state provided Greyhound bus that would take him home. Over the years, he accepted the fact that this day would probably never happen. Finally, it had.

While walking to his seat, and looking at people's faces on the bus, he realized how happy he was not to be surrounded by those that abide by a code of, "keep with your own and always carry a knife."

As he sat down, he realized, maybe he didn't agree with Sartyr. Maybe other people weren't hell? He thought about the last eighteen month that were spent in solitary confinement. How all he wanted was to see his mother's face, his little brother's face, the faces of strangers on the street, any face other than the face of the guards he'd become accustomed to seeing. Their faces weren't human. They were more like automated machines wearing a perpetual scowl of contempt.

They didn't consider the fact that, if he hadn't done what he had to do that day on the yard, that one quick act of defense that landed him in the hole for three years, he wouldn't be here right now riding this bus to a new life. A life where there wasn't the need to practice "The Art of War" philosophies or the teachings of "The 48 Laws of Power," to survive. A life, where he could forget the diagrams that taught him where to stick a blade in a man for a quick kill.

He could begin to put in practice the Taoist and Buddhist teachings he'd studied in isolation. He came to believe that there's a life force flowing through every organism on the planet. In Taoism they call it "Chi." Breezy referred to it as "One," referencing "one love." He adopted the deeper meaning to this phrase so that whenever someone said it to him in parting, it would remind him, on a level no one was aware of, that all things were made of and breath the same life force, and that a man could transform himself by being aware of and in tune with it.

He had to remind himself that change was possible. He had to believe that not getting his third strike was possible. He had to believe that he was meant for more than crime, prison, and recidivism's trap.

As he rode the bus north, staring out the window at rows of cornfields that reminded him of rows of naked men lined up and forced to bend over, spread 'em, and cough, he couldn't help but think that his personal age of reason was about to unfold.

He hadn't given up hope. He didn't believe that he would be relegated to the life of a career criminal like his father and older brothers. He knew the universe had bigger plans for him, he could feel it.

He had read what Joseph Campbell said about the mythological hero, and it made sense. Just like Odysseus, he'd been sent away from home, forced by fate to fight his way through life or death scenarios, battling his own cyclops', overcoming siren songs, and walking through the land of giants. He had fought the battles and won. He was now coming out the other end, war torn with scars, but victorious and transformed, a hero.

He was now thirty miles from home and about to embark on the next phase of his transition. One where he could put everything he'd learned into action.

He'd educated himself. First getting his G.E.D. and continuing until he'd obtained his bachelor's degree. He was able to study for hours, uninterrupted in his cell. He even managed to be Valedictorian of the college from where his degree was accredited. He maintained a solid 4.0 the entire time he was a student/inmate.

As the bus pulled into the downtown terminal, he was riding a pink cloud of excitement, buzzing with the renewed energy of a man raised from the dead.

His plan was to get a job counseling at-risk youth. Teach them, before it was too late, not to do the stupid shit he grew up doing. Show them a different formula for living. Help them get off the streets and out the game. Preach the importance of education and warn them where they would end up if they stayed on the path he was getting off. He wanted to do this in an attempt to right the wrongs of his past.

He stepped off the bus, carrying the paper bag he was given for his belongings- deodorant, toothbrush, notebook, pen, a copy of The I Ching, and a spare set of kicks- everything he had to show after eleven years up state.

While looking up at the city's skyscrapers, taking in the traffic and people rushing around him, feeling hopeful for what lay ahead, he heard a voice, "Yo, Breezy!"

When he turned around, before he saw a face, he heard a gun fire three shots and felt the sudden burn of bullets rip through his chest.

He fell to the ground, staring up at blue sky, gasping for air through gargled blood as a man walked up, stood over him and said, "You killed my brother,

Motherfucker! Think I'd forget?" Then the man spit on him.

Breezy was unsure exactly who this act of vengeance was for, he had ended more than one life. But he didn't dwell on this. Like a true student of Eastern philosophy and a man filled with dharma, he thought to himself, "Karma keeps chaos in order."

Scott Wozniak is an award-winning spoken-word artist, poet, short story writer, chaos enthusiast, and champion monkey-wrench thrower. He lives in Oregon.

JOURNEY OF LOSS
Danielle McCoy

She hesitated for a moment on the edge of the swamp. She had lost much along her journey to this place, but she knew that the losses ahead were a different kind altogether. It wasn't the kind of decision to be made lightly. Still, she wanted to let go of this life, that had taken and taken from her, but never seemed to give. She found a tree where the ground was still solid and left a small pack there on the ground. She was here to lose herself, so these last mementos were an anchor she couldn't afford. Steeling her resolve, she took the first step into the unknown.

Stepping into the swamp was like stepping into a dream. Time seemed to move too slowly, and the landscape she passed never seemed to change. Her limbs burned from fighting against the sucking mud almost instantly, so even her exhaustion wasn't a real indicator of how far she had come. It wasn't even resolve that kept her going, just that dream-like feeling that moving forward was the only possible action.

And in this endless haze of motion, she found that she had arrived. She knew that this was the place as only someone who has wandered an interminable amount of time in a waking dream can know. This was the place because it was - that was just how it was. In this moment of lucidity, she realized that she had lost every material thing she had ever had. She didn't remember when she last ate, how long she had been walking barefoot, or when her clothes had been torn to tatters. These were inconsequential to the swamp, and therefore inconsequential to her.

She shed the last remains of her clothing and stood with only herself left to lose.

Before her was a tree. Trees were everywhere in the swamp, and this tree was not different from them. It was everything the other trees were, but somehow more - more like the other trees than they were themselves. This tree was the heart of the swamp and the place where the dreamlike atmosphere was thickest. In that one moment of clarity, she wasn't sure if she was looking at a tree, or if it was only the essential essence of a tree that was being projected to her. The difference didn't really seem to matter, and she abandoned the clarity to sink deeper into the miasma of the swamp.

That was, after all, why she was here.

At the base of the tree was a hollow, and she pushed herself inside. She found herself in a chamber made of twisted roots. It was not large, but far larger than had seemed possible from outside. The opening back to the swamp was nowhere in evidence, but she had lost any desire to go back so this didn't concern her anyway. Tendrils hung from the ceiling, brushing around her body as she moved to the center of the space.

Much like the journey from the edge of the swamp, her sense of time was distorted here. She watched the tendrils grow and wind their way around her body, but she couldn't tell if it was happening quickly or if she was merely watching them grow at a normal pace. She had lost the feeling of the natural functions of her body. She felt no need to breathe, eat, or sleep.

She felt no urgency as the tendrils enveloped her, covering more and more of her skin.

Soon, she could no longer move. A glimmer of thought rose up in her mind that the end was near, and soon she could sink into oblivion. The tendrils rippled around her as the thought blossomed, and then was plucked from her brain. No, she suddenly knew, if she had wanted oblivion, she should have slit her wrists and been done with it. She had come here, to lose herself in this place, and a peaceful descent into nothing was not part of that.

Her body, covered in tendrils, was being remade. Rootlets replaced muscle, bark replaced skin, swamp water began to flow in her veins instead of blood. And her consciousness, devoid of desire or ambition, experienced each change in intimate detail. It wasn't painless, but the pain was incidental, not by design. This wasn't intended to be torture. She felt the intertwining of herself with the swamp. Even as her body was remade of the stuff of the swamp, her mind was also sifted and remade. Everything she had been was still there - held in the swamp until needed, even as other parts were added to her, to make her what the swamp needed her to be. That was her last loss - losing the essence of who she was to the swamp, to become as the swamp made her.

Like emerging from a chrysalis, she stepped out of the tree at the heart of the swamp. Another step took her to the edge where she had entered. The entire swamp was part of her now, or she just a part of its larger whole, and movement within its borders was as easy as thought. She looked little different than when she had embarked on her journey of loss. She saw the little pack at the base of a tree, hidden amongst the growth of unknown seasons. She remembered it and all the invaluable trinkets it contained, memories of the life she had lost, but they weren't her memories anymore. They were just a drop in the vast ocean of the memories that had been absorbed into the consciousness of the swamp. She left it there under the overgrowth, lost at edge of where the ground was still solid. The emissary of the swamp moved outward; her purpose finally clear.

Danielle McCoy spends her days working in retail customer service, and her evenings with her dogs and children. She has dabbled in writing on and off her whole life, but only recently moved towards submitting to small publishers.

SLOT ZOMBIES
Brian Rouff

"Hey Boss," Gabriel Ortiz said, "come on over here. You need to see this."

Tom Stafford, head of security for downtown Vegas' Lucky Cuss casino/hotel, hoisted himself with a groan from his genuine imitation leatherette desk chair (held together by matching brown duct tape) and trudged over to the bank of surveillance monitors where Ortiz stood. "This better be good," Stafford said. "I was just about to take a whiz."

"Then you needed to get up regardless."

"Not necessarily." Stafford rocked back and forth from foot to foot. "What's so damned interesting anyway?"

Ortiz pointed to the screen, indicating a skinny gray-haired Asian woman in a safari print mumuu. "See this old broad feeding nickels into the *Shuffling Dead* slot on carousel 13?"

Stafford frowned. "Yeah? Looks like every other granny we get in this dump."

"That's where you're wrong. I just got a call from Johnson on the floor. Said she hasn't gotten out of her seat since he started his shift."

"You called me over for that? I'd write you up if I could find my pen." Christ. Eighteen years in this racket and it's come to this. If only he hadn't told the truth on question 47 of the Metro police entrance exam, things might have been different.

Ortiz continued, "And Miller said exactly the same thing. So, I backed up the video. She's been sitting there for 27 hours. Straight. Hasn't moved a muscle except to push that damned button."

"Probably wearing the giant economy size Depends," Stafford said with a shrug.

Ortiz wheeled around to face his boss. "Except she hasn't ordered a drink, lit a cigarette, lifted a cheek to fart, nothin'. What you make of it?"

"I'd say she's a good customer. Is she ahead?"

"Up and down. Hasn't had to dip into her purse, if that's what you mean."

"Well, the house always wins in the end. And that's all that counts. Now get outta my way before I water your ficus," Stafford said, pretending to unzip.

Ortiz didn't budge, blocking Stafford's path with his ex-lineman's frame. "We should have medical take a look at her. Just to cover our asses."

"Okay, have it your way. Although it's not my *ass* I'm worried about."

Charles "Doc" Merritt threw back a shot of bottom shelf bourbon and shuddered. It went down like molten glass. "Hit me again, my comely serving wench" he said, slapping a couple of soggy singles on the bar. Before he could do any further damage to his 67-year-old system, he felt a beefy hand on his shoulder. Wincing, he turned to focus on the hand's owner, a stocky moon-faced fellow with a porn star moustache.

"Officer Ortiz, to what do I owe the exquisite pleasure?"

"Doc, how many times I gotta tell you about drinking on duty?"

Merritt blinked. "I don't recall us ever engaging in that particular conversation."

Ortiz grinned despite himself. "You can't recall your own damned name half the time. Get off that stool if you can and follow me. We got a lady might need your attention; God help her."

Merritt stood, swayed, steadied himself and put one wobbly foot in front of the other all the way to the slot carousel where the elderly Asian lady continued to sit like a statue.

After a quick briefing from Ortiz, Merritt leaned in and said, "Excuse me, madam, Charles Merritt at your service. I'm the house physician. May I have a word with you?"

No response. Merritt cleared his throat and tried again, louder this time. "My good woman, the people who run this establishment are concerned for your welfare. I must insist you stop playing and speak to me this instant."

Still nothing. Merritt extended a shaky hand and gave her arm a gentle tug, just enough to get her attention. That's when he knew he'd made a terrible mistake.

"She bit me!" Merritt howled like a wounded dog. "The bitch bit me." He sat on a stained plastic chair bathed in the sick green light of the casino infirmary, gingerly applying an antiseptic wipe to a nasty chunk taken out of his right wrist.

"Quit your whining," Stafford said. "It's not the worst thing that's happened to you around here."

Merritt had to agree. During his time at the Lucky Cuss, he'd been sneezed on, puked on, peed on, shit on, and bled on. There wasn't a form of bodily discharge that hadn't found its way onto, and perhaps into, his person. It was a minor miracle he hadn't contracted AIDS or Hep C. His football-sized liver was something else entirely, but at least that was self-inflicted. Small consolation as he placed a large gauze pad over his newly acquire souvenir, now growing redder and angrier by the second. Merritt knew the human mouth harbored more bacteria than that of most animals; with his luck he'd be fighting a raging infection by morning. He'd have to remember to write himself a scrip for a Z-Pak and hit the Walgreen's on East Flamingo on his way home. In the meantime, he eyed a bottle of isopropyl alcohol and it was as though Stafford could read his mind. "You can't drink that stuff, Doc. You'll go blind. I'll have Stacy bring up a bottle of that rotgut you're so fond of."

"As long as it's on the house, maybe she could favor me with a Wild Turkey. Just this once?"

"Just this once," Stafford said. "Besides, we got more important things to talk about. Like what to do about that crazy old broad."

The old broad in question rested quietly in a locked holding facility in the casino basement, pushing the button on a non-existent slot machine. It had taken Ortiz and two other guards a full three minutes to subdue her, mainly because they were trying to avoid her surprisingly powerful choppers. Pepper spray just pissed her off. Cuffing was out of the question. Only when Davis sent her false teeth flying with a well-placed baton to the mouth (they landed squarely in the middle of a nearby craps table with nary a glance from the regulars) did they feel confident enough to wrestle her to the floor.

"So, what do we do with her?" Stafford asked. "Metro or UMC?" Meaning the cops or the hospital. Vegas didn't have its own version of Bellevue psychiatric, although lord knows it needed one.

"We could flip a coin," Merritt said. "But if we make the wrong decision, I might lose my license."

"You got a license?"

"Last I checked. I hate to say it, but I'd better have a closer look at her. Officer Ortiz, would you please accompany me? And bring two of your largest companions."

Ortiz and the companions, as it turned out, were unnecessary. The woman had returned to her former semi-vegetative state, docile enough (after some cautious prodding with a particularly long cotton swab) for Merritt to perform a perfunctory exam, the results of which made him crave the rest of the Wild Turkey. Just to be sure, he went through the routine a second time, pleased to know he could still act like a real doctor when the situation warranted. Now if it weren't for that damned twitch in his right hand . . .

"What's the story?" Stafford asked when Merritt and his helpers returned to the security room. "You look like shit, by the way. After we're done here, why don't you call it a night?"

Merritt plopped himself onto a metal folding chair. "I'm most appreciative of your concern for my health and well-being," he said, knocking back an enormous swig from the bottle of bourbon.

"At this juncture, our guest downstairs is technically, how shall I put this . . . dead."

"Jesus Christ, when the hell did that happen?" He envisioned lawsuits, weeping relatives and stacks of paperwork plunging his life into new depths of misery.

"Based on her body temperature of 83.7, I'd say roughly ten hours ago."

"Quit your clowning Doc. The faster we wrap this up, the faster we both get out of here."

"I've never been more serious in my life. There's no pulse, no blood pressure, no pupillary response to light. I checked twice. Ask Mr. Ortiz."

"He's telling the truth Boss." Ortiz crossed himself with one hand while fingering the gold crucifix around his neck with the other.

Stafford looked like a man listening to a used car salesman. "Assuming this isn't a case of the DTs, how do you account for the imaginary button pushing? What is she, some kind of slot zombie?" His laugh was part snort, all derision.

Merritt plowed ahead.

"There are a number of pharmacological substances known to mirror morbidity, most notably tetrodotoxin. The Haitians are famous for it. But the more logical explanation is reflex action. Cadavers have historically been known to exhibit reflexive behavior, although not to this extent. There may be a small vestigial part of her brain still active."

Stafford rubbed his already bloodshot eyes. "So, I guess we call the morgue then? Ortiz, you got positive ID on the, uh, deceased?"

Ortiz shook his bowling ball-sized noggin. "Nothing in her purse except a couple dozen Wet Wipes, some loose singles and a bunch of rolls from the buffet. Buttered."

"May I offer a suggestion?" Merritt said. "I'd like to keep her on ice for a few more hours of observation. This could be a once-in-a-lifetime phenomenon." He flashed on an image of his byline in the *New England Journal of Medicine*. His hand was flopping around like a one-legged cricket and he jammed it deep in his pocket. The hand could wait. There was nothing more important than the dead Jane Doe in the basement.

Tom Stafford, already sweating through his white dress shirt, marched to the board room podium like a man facing a firing squad. "G-g-gentleman," he said to the Lucky Cuss executive team, "we have a problem."

CEO Arthur Morgante, he of the perfect hair and teeth, jumped in. "Problems are just opportunities in disguise." Morgante, a typical Las Vegas success story, had started out a decade earlier playing piano in the casino lounge before somehow magically acquiring controlling interest in the property. He hadn't sunk a dime into it since, bleeding the place dry while letting it devolve into downtown's most notorious shithole. What remained of the carpeting would feel right at home in a toxic waste dump, while the billows of unfiltered air made second-hand smoke look like pure oxygen.

Opportunities, Stafford thought. *Wait'll you hear this one.* With that he laid out the details of the previous night's activities, including a few new developments that included Doc Merritt, Gabriel Ortiz and half the security staff, all sporting fresh bite marks, sharing guest quarters with Patient Zero. And pushing those damned imaginary buttons.

When he finally ran out of breath, Stafford scanned the faces of the assembled execs, staring at him wide-eyed and wide-mouthed, resembling bottom feeders pulled up from the deep. Nobody wanted to risk being the first to comment for fear of ridicule or worse. Instead, they waited for Morgante to weigh in, at which time they could nod their heads approvingly and chirp in agreement. And weigh in he did, although not in the way they expected.

"That miserable fucking Wexler. Okay, everybody out. Out!" he said, pounding his fist on the table. No sooner had the door clicked shut than Morgante punched a number into his cell phone, his hands shaking in rage.

"Neil, Arthur Morgante. We've got a situation here and it's your fault, you lying piece of shit."

"Wait a minute, wait a minute," said Neil R. Wexler, CEO of Universal Gaming Technologies, makers of 80 percent of all slot games in Las Vegas including the prototype *Shuffling Dead* progressive. "What the hell are you talking about?"

"You know goddamned well what I'm talking about. The chip you installed in that fancy new machine of yours, the one you gave us the 'exclusive' test market on. That's some favor you did me. It's turning my people into zombies."

"Impossible. We've never had a product that exceeded so many of our quality control protocols. It's simply designed to impact the human neural network in a very subtle way"

"Subtle my ass." Wexler started to protest but Morgante cut him off. "Now you listen to me. You fix this. I don't care how you do it, but you fix it. Or my friends in Kansas City are going to pay you and your family a nice long visit."

Morgante slammed the cell on the table, ending the conversation and the phone at the same time. Storming across the room, he flung open the heavy wooden door, causing his assembled flunkies to scatter like pigeons.

"Dolan, get in here."

Like the casino itself, PR Director Mike Dolan had seen better days. But he could still rise to the occasion when the occasion demanded. That and working cheap kept him in Morgante's stable of has-beens.

"Word gets out and we're all history," Morgante said after filling Dolan in. "I don't think any of us want to hit the streets at our age. Mike, how we gonna spin this?"

Dolan's head was already spinning. It went hand-in-hand with the churning in his gut. "Well, here's what we know," he said in a voice that quavered more than he was hoping for. "The Asian woman is a Jane Doe, no ID, right? So, likely nobody's looking for her. How about Merritt? Anyone give two shits about him?"

"Nah. An ex-wife or two somewhere. No kids that I know of."

"And Ortiz?"

Morgante glanced over his shoulder reflexively and whispered, "Illegal. The rest of the guards too. Completely off the books."

"And as long as nobody bothers them, they just sit there pushing buttons?"

"Whether there's a machine or not."

Dolan held his hands out in triumph. "So, there you go."

"There I go what?"

"Your answer. Stick them in front of those newfangled slots, set the machines for tournament play so they don't need money, and leave them the hell alone. They don't drink, don't smoke and won't bother anyone. And they certainly won't smell worse than any of your regulars. The perfect shills if you ask me. Before you know it, this joint'll be packed with real customers. Paying ones. Because people want to hang out where the action is."

It was as though the sun rose on Morgante's face. "And they work for free. Dolan, you're a genius. Let me use your phone."

As Dolan pondered the prospect of a raise and maybe even some time off for good behavior, Morgante made his call.

"Neil, it's me. Forget what I said. Order me up another dozen slots."

Brian Rouff was born in Detroit, raised in Southern California and has lived in Las Vegas since 1981, which makes him a long timer by local standards. When he's not writing articles, short stories, screenplays and Las Vegas novels such as Dice Angels, Money Shot, and The House Always Wins, he runs Imagine

Communications, a marketing and public relations firm. On a personal note, Brian is married with two grown daughters and five grandchildren. In his spare time, he enjoys reading, playing guitar, and an occasional visit to the casino buffet lines.

THE SAD PART
Dan Provost

The Sad Part

I wanted to die.

Looking out my window was the closest I dared myself to integrate with society. There was a cold, sadness in the pit of my being. I knew I could not believe that things outside my bubble were real. Every day was that black and white pursuit—that desire to be gone from the thing called existence.

Did I have the balls to do it?

I know I digress—but it all ties into the same question, doesn't it? Having the desire to leave this thing called life and being able to physically perform the act. Understanding that I lacked the guts to even to step out the door most of the time, I realized that this might be a huh...huh...*inside job* where hanging, overdose on my depression pills, or cutting my wrist would be realistic options to end it all.

Ha...I digress again. The times I did go out—my being was filled with anxiety, sadness and fear. I usually went to bars—hoping to get out of my mind a little by drinking and listening to music. I usually sat alone, not saying much and pouring money into the juke box listening to lyrics that I enjoyed from another lifetime ago.

Isolated among the isolated as it were...again funny, so fucking funny.

John Berryman

John Berryman once said, "Life is boring". He was right. Damn Skippy he was right. Where do you find a sense of purpose? An attached memo within your soul claiming that you have the inevitable right to live? To exist? It wasn't my idea to be here…I wanted no process in the act of "making a living" or "observing the life around me". I wanted to tread on a different plane—a non-secular alternative of communicating, of wanting, of companionship…I did not think these thoughts at a frantic pace, nor do I expect anything to come out of my desires…

I cannot fully explain what my desires are…
Can you?

Hatred and Being Polite

Besides going to the local pub, the few occasions I chose to mingle with anybody remotely representing society was out of necessity…but a paradox, nevertheless.

Part of me wanted out—out of life, out of existence; out of anything that resembled what I was seeing outside my window.

But living on depression and two-dollar crackers left me stomach to gurgle, so I would, on occasion go to the grocery store. It was always a miserable experience…Cramped with old ladies and mothers with uncontrollable children always getting in the way.

My mind was one of justified murder—you are in my way grandma; your kids are wailing in my ear mom…get the fuck away from me or I will destroy you by sheer will.

But these were just thoughts, desires that I envisioned but would never act upon. I would be polite, always saying 'excuse me" or grin in an accepted but haughty way.

I would physically pick up my cart if the aisles were packed with gabby mothers that refused to believe they were blocking my attempt to get a frozen dinner.

Putting it down...they always would look at me and mutter "oh sorry" and I would smile and tell them— "It's OK, no problem" when inside, I wanted to kick them in the tits.

Their continued conversation about absolutely nothing would leave me to shutter. What if these women just melted away due to my will...my wants, my needs? But I realize this will not happen—so I do not pray to God, do not spit and slander their very existence, do not wish them any unhappiness or pain externally...I just go about my own way—grab my chicken pot pie and leave the situation completely...Aware of what is going on in my gut but not reacting or responding to any emotional outburst.

It is to weep...

Too Much of a Pussy to Do It

I will continue to whine about suicide, but will I commit the act? The reason, I'm afraid of what is on the other side. Living in darkness for eternity is not what I look forward to. But is this living?

Who am I to say...Who am I to say anything about anything...Mothers raise babies to grow up as solid, righteous members of society, but what is society anyways? Just a bunch of programed robots who...oh, you know the question...but the answers can come cheap sometimes...They may come in a retirement plan, a drink in France, a good drunk at a dive bar—or the end of a knife. I know, deep down—I am a pussy and probably not dare to bring the blade to my wrist. To those who do...you have the mental stability of something that many can't or will not comprehend.

You see the worthlessness of this dice game, an understanding of the being engulfed in total sooty blackness. It is awful, it is non-forgiving and it leads to any action that will lead to escape.

God, do I hate myself...and I have said this all before...

Music
Fair alternative to being at a barbershop...
Literature
Fair alternative to being at a funeral...
Sex
Fair alternative to walking your dog...

Wilfred Owen

On depression and the thought of suicide: *It was not despair, or terror, it was more terrible than terror, for it was a blindfold look, and without expression, like a dead rabbit.*

It will never be painted, and no actor will ever seize it. And to describe it, I think I must go back and be with them...

I am not original in my dilemma...That is what sometimes pisses me off about disillusionment and destruction...Watch the anti-heroes walk down the street with the glazed, blank look...Does it pertain to you? Do you seize the *affliction* of non-life that staggers with every step?

The typical labeled names I was given by doctors, neighbors, and strangers: dejected, aloof, self-involved, suffering from suicidal ideation...all whims of the internal terror and obsessive pain that is suffered. I sit in my chair and stare ad nauseum at a picture of my dead sister, my dead parents...Dead—all dead.

You have won today Wilfred...I will find my gun, find the knife, take the pills...If Christ could have his Gethsemane...

I can have my own audience with whatever lies after...I will walk, isolated into some cheap, wooded area some see as beautiful...I see it as just another place to overrate nature...Another place, for one more time to flash that *"blindfold look"* around at invisible peers who, after I am finished—well continue to peer into...into absolutely nothing...

Then, the questions will go on and on and on...Me—

I will know the answer.

Am I still a pussy?

Dan Provost's words have appeared throughout the small press world for years. He is the author of ten books, some of which include: A Quiet Learning Curve (shared with Aleathia Drehmer), Weathered Woman, The Southside of Agony, You've Gotta Let it Go Before it Takes You Over (shared with Paul Koniecki and Abigail Beaudelle) and Wear Brighter Colors. Dan lives in Berlin, New Hampshire with his wife Laura and their Bichon Frisce, Bella.

TWO TURTLE DOVES
Richard Wall

My first guitar saved my life. I wish now that I'd never set eyes on it.

It was 1973.

I was on my way to step out in front of an express train. I knew a place where I could walk onto the track at the very last second, giving the driver no time to brake.

I had it all planned.

When you're an underdeveloped, bespectacled, thirteen-year-old, stammering ginger bookworm, you become the target of choice for every thug, wanker and dickhead looking for a docile recipient for their anger issues.

Dave Scott was Dickhead-in-Chief, with Alex, his twin brother, a very able lieutenant. They were two years older, and their joint mission in life was to seek me out and kick the living shit out of me at every given opportunity. This they did with an amount of pleasure, imagination and attention to detail that was terrifying.

Not that I was a stranger to the dark side of life. I had a brother in the army. Hard as nails he was. But he was killed in Northern Ireland, which caused my dad to drink himself to death, leaving me and my mum on our own. Victims don't attract friends, and with no one to turn to, I lived in my head.

Welcome to my world.

Bullies take your mind to places where rules don't exist. Alone with your thoughts, a maelstrom of anger fuels your imagination. You fantasize about revenge; a hammer to the temple, a knitting needle pushed slowly into the ear, a razor blade dragged across an eyeball, bending a finger back until it snaps with a loud crack. Make them scream, make them bleed, make them beg for mercy. In your mind you're ready for them. Until the next time. When you turn the corner, and they're waiting, and you piss yourself with fear because you haven't got a hammer, or a knitting needle, or the muscle, expertise or bravery to fight back, and you know damn well that it will be you begging for mercy.

Soon after that your mind tells you that you're worthless, and with no case for the defense you make an appointment for a meeting with the business end of a speeding locomotive.

I was on my way to that meeting when I spotted the guitar propped up next to some dustbins outside the Oxfam shop.

Up until then I had never seen a guitar up close, much less had any desire to play, but when I saw that cheap, wooden acoustic, with nylon strings and plastic tuning pegs, something about it, temporarily distracted me from the dark side of my brain.

There would be another express tomorrow.

I took the guitar home, borrowed a tuition book from the library, and set about devoting every spare minute to practicing. In a very short time, I reached the point where I needed something better.

Our neighbour next door-but-one, was a rep for a Mail Order Catalogue. Mum had borrowed a copy and left it on the kitchen table. I was flipping through it when I found the "Musical Instruments" page.

That's when I saw it.

"El Diablo" was a Chinese copy of a Gibson SG electric guitar. It had accentuated double cutaways that resembled devil's horns. The body was painted in a red so vivid that it reminded me of a stab wound and branded the outline of Satan's head behind my eyelids every time that I blinked.

I spent an hour staring at it (I even took a Polaroid photograph of the page, which I carried everywhere), obsession growing inside me like a tumour as I pored over the technical specifications whilst ignoring the reality.

The price was an eye-watering £250. Even the lowest weekly payment, spread over three years was beyond my meagre budget. Asking mum was out of the question. We didn't have pot to piss in, and an electric guitar was at the bottom of the priority list.

That night I dreamt of it. We were centre-stage in a dark, stinking dive-bar, playing to a crowd of slavering, writhing and fornicating scarlet demons. El Diablo screamed out a blistering, elongated siren-call laden with reverb and feedback.

As I played, the room began to shudder, the dirt floor erupting ripe mud pustules through which corpses scrabbled from their graves, stood upright, and then got their bad selves on down to the groove. El Diablo screamed louder then dive-bombed to a heavy, low-down 12-bar blues. Demons grunted like rutting pigs, shitting everywhere as the guttural power chords and driving bass line resonated deep within their bowels.

In the midst of this rancid hellhole, one of demons separated itself from the undulating mass, turned and lumbered towards me, its breath inundating my world with unholy stench as it morphed into Keith Richards.

"You get that axe, it's gonna change your life," Keith growled. "How much of a deposit would you need to afford the payments?"

A corpse shuffled across the stage, strips of rotting material flapping and dangling from its bones, wisps of dirty grey hair creeping from beneath the rim of a filthy top hat. As it drew closer, scraps of desiccated facial muscle twitched in an obscene representation of a grin as the corpse laid its bony hand on my shoulder.

"Today is Friday," it croaked. "People pay their bills on Friday."

I erupted from the nightmare, my pajamas wringing with sweat, my heart thumping as I switched on the light and waited for the images to fade.

The catalogue was on the floor where I'd left it. The photograph of El Diablo wiggling her curves at me, looking every bit as seductive as a Playboy Centerfold.

At the back of the catalogue was about ten pages of small print. I speed-read through to the payment terms and calculated that a 20% deposit would halve the weekly payments over three years. Putting El Diablo well within my limited means.

All I had to do was find fifty pounds.

It was dark when my alarm went off, and cold when I slipped out of bed. Outside, the clear sky glistened with stars, the ground with frost and icy treachery.

I was halfway along my paper round when from behind I heard the familiar clinking bottles and low whirring electric hum of Sid Davies' milk float.

Sid gave a cheery wave as he drove past and then steered across the road to stop outside a block of flats.

I watched him step out of the cab and reach for a crate of milk bottles.

I watched him heft the crate onto his shoulder, and then turn towards the flats.

I watched him take three steps, and then his feet shot from under him.

I saw his head hit the pavement, heard his skull crack through the crash of breaking glass.

When I reached him, Sid wasn't moving. Blood poured from his ears, running along the camber of the pavement, mixing with spilt milk to create a grotesque strawberry milkshake in the gutter.

I remembered my brother telling me that if someone is bleeding from the ears, then it's not a good sign.

I knelt down and felt Sid's neck for a pulse like my brother had shown me.

Nothing.

I grabbed his wrist.

Nothing.

Sid always wore a battered leather satchel on a thin strap slung over his left shoulder. The satchel lay to one side, the flap was open and in the pool of sodium light I could see banknotes inside. Lots of banknotes.

"It's Friday. Everyone pays their bills on Friday."

"You get that axe, it's gonna change your life."

I looked up and down the street. It was still early, still no sign of any movement. No lights coming on. No curtains twitching. No one around.

I looked back at Sid. Checked his pulse again.

Nothing.

My heart pounded as I slipped my hand inside the satchel, grabbed fistfuls of notes and stuffed them frantically into my paper sack.

"Whu...whu...whu..."

I stifled a scream as a hand grabbed my wrist. Sid was awake, gripping my arm, his cheeks puffing and deflating as he blew strange words into the cold morning air.

I leaned over him. "Can you hear me, Sid?"

"Whu...whu...whu..."

"Do you know who I am, Sid?"

"Whu...whu...whu..."

His left foot began to quiver, and then shudder violently.

"Sid?"

By now his head lay in a pool of blood, his eyes staring wildly. I pried his fingers from my wrist.

"Do you know where you are, Sid?"

"Whu...whu...whu..."

I looked around. Still no sign of anyone.

El Diablo flashed into my vision. Its body pulsing like arterial blood.

"You get that axe, it's gonna change your life."

I took a deep breath, grabbed Sid's head in both hands, lifted it and then hammered it onto the pavement.

I felt something give, like the shattering of an eggshell.

"Whuwhuwhuwhu."

Sid's breathing became ragged.

I lifted his head again. This time I put the weight of my body behind it, smashing it down with all the force I could muster. Again, and again and again.

Crack.

Crack.

Crack.

Sid's eyeballs rolled upwards, he gave a final clattering gasp, and then fell silent.

I smashed his head once more, saw something ooze from the back of his skull.

By now I was panting, my arms aching.

I stood up and looked around again. Still nobody about.

I stepped over Sid's body and carried on with my paper round, pulling banknotes out of my sack and stuffing them into my pockets.

Nobody saw me walking away.

Back at home, I laid the cash out on my bed.

One hundred and twenty-five pounds.

Fast Forward to 1975.

I was still underweight, still stammering, still short-sighted, and still ginger. But I could play the guitar just like ringing a bell.

Hours and hours of finger-shredding practice was finally beginning to pay off. I could play pretty much anything, any style. I had inherited my brother's record collection and developed a preference for early electric blues, and everything by the Rolling Stones up to Exile on Main St. (the last album he bought before the IRA blew him up).

The bullying had lessened somewhat. Encounters were fewer, but no less violent. Going out was safer, but the effects lingered on and my mind was still feeding me sinister thoughts.

El Diablo was my comfort blanket, soaking up my anger, calming my fears and converting my bleak thoughts into sweet tones. Whatever mood I was in, she made me sound good, and when I thought the voices in my head weren't listening, I would daydream of a playing in a band.

The Turtle Doves were formed at my school in your standard rock group formation: lead singer, two guitarists, bassist and drummer.
Mick Taylor, the lead singer was a tall, skinny narcissist who thought he was Mick Jagger. He really wasn't.

Dave Scott was the original lead guitarist. The very same spiteful, loudmouth bastard who made my formative years a living hell.
Rhythm guitarist was Alex Scott, Dave's twin brother and partner in crime.

Bassist was Jimmy Morton. Dedicated to music. Later on, Jimmy co-wrote all the songs with me.

The drummer was Tom Cornwell. Legend.

I'd watched them practice a few times at school and noticed that cracks were beginning to appear. Jimmy wanted the band to record original material (he was a prolific songwriter), whereas Dave and Alex insisted on playing covers because they couldn't be arsed to put in the work to create something new. No one else in the band could write music and so Jimmy was outvoted every time. After one particularly memorable argument, the practice session ended with the Scott brothers storming off.

I walked out of school that afternoon to find them leaning against a wall, passing a fag back and forth. Dave's face twisted into a sneer.

"What are you looking at, you little cunt?"

"Nothing," I said.

I didn't see the first punch, just felt the explosion on my face and the familiar taste of blood in my mouth. The second punch put me on the floor, after that, all I could do was curl up tight and try and protect my head against the volley of kicks from Dave and his bastard brother.

I heard shouting, then a scuffle, and then the kicking stopped, and I was being lifted to my feet.

"Four-eyed ginger twat." The Scott brothers laughed as they swaggered away.

"Are you alright?" Jimmy looked genuinely concerned.

I sniffed back tears. "I th-think so."

"Pair of wankers," said Jimmy.

He stepped back. "I saw you watching us practice," he said. "You like music?"

I nodded. "I p-play guitar," I said.

I showed him the latest Polaroid of El Diablo.

"Nice," said Jimmy. "Listen. We're playing at the Rose and Lion on Saturday, why don't you come along?

I'll make sure those two won't bother you. Maybe we can hear you play?"

"M-maybe," I said.

"See you on Saturday, then." Jimmy turned and walked away.

When he'd gone, I stared for a long time at the picture.

By now the Polaroid was about six months old, the glossy paper well-worn and creased, the image beginning to fade. But as I stared at the picture the colour of El Diablo seemed to become more vivid.

"Burning like the flames of hell."

The voice made me jump. Its sinister tone suggesting another kicking was inbound, but when I looked around there was no one there.

The Rose and Lion was a down-at-heel pub in a shabby side street that led to a small park and kids' playground.

The gig didn't go well. A burly, shaven-headed punter made his way to the stage and began to heckle Dave. At first Dave tried to ignore him, but the shaven-headed guy was relentless and seemed to know which buttons to press.

Dave stopped playing, grabbed his guitar by the neck and hit the floor swinging. Punches were traded, Dave was pulled away, and Shaven-Headed Guy was bundled out of the pub.

The next morning Jimmy turned up at my house.

"We're looking for a new guitarist," he said.

Jimmy told me that after leaving the pub, the Shaven-Headed Guy waited outside. Witnesses saw him grab Dave and frog march him into the park.

Next morning, Dave was discovered near the swings. Every single bone in his body had been systematically and expertly broken.

A couple of weeks later, on a Friday afternoon, I went to visit Dave in hospital. He was out of Intensive Care and in a room on his own. Encased in a body cast, and hanging from traction wires, he looked like a wounded marionette.

I walked up to the bed and leaned in close. The bruising on his face had ripened to a midnight blue, with patchy clouds of sickly yellow. His broken jaw was wired shut, rendering his trapped words unintelligible.

Swollen, bloodshot eyes stared back at me, first with anger, then uncertainty, and then widening in fear as I licked his face, dragging my tongue from his chin to his forehead.

I leaned closer, to whisper in his ear.

"Burn in hell, you piece of shit."

I grabbed a pillow from an armchair next to the bed, placed it over Dave's face and pushed down hard.

It was over in seconds. The bed shook violently at first, and then calmed, and then silence.

I looked up at the sound of a scratch-flare, and the smell of burning tobacco.

Sid, the milkman, stood in the corner of the room, dragging on a Woodbine. His pallid, death-mask creased into a grin as smoke poured from his nostrils and mouth.

"It's Friday," he said. "People pay their bills on Friday."

Sid winked at me. "When they lifted me up," he said. "My brains fell out of the back of my head. Have a look."

He turned around. Jagged edges of skull framed a gaping hole in the back of his head, like a windowpane after a brick has gone through it. Sid turned to face me, and then nodded at Dave's body. "He's on his way. Probably burning as we speak."

His cheeks hollowed as he drew on the Woodbine. "You better go," he said.

I put the pillow back on the chair. When I looked up, Sid was gone.

I took a moment to stroke Dave's head, felt myself smile as I whispered, "Fuck you," and then I walked out of the room.

I joined the band. Jimmy and I began writing together, and gradually we built up a decent repertoire of hard-driving songs.
Without his thug twin for back up, Alex left me alone. But he still hated my guts, and I hated his. I bided my time.

In 1976, Malcom Maclaren's Monkees hit the UK like a lightning bolt, sparking a wildfire that swept across the country.

By 1977 our back catalogue captured the zeitgeist perfectly and we were soon compared with The Clash and The Stranglers.

Our name began to spread. A demo tape played by John Peel begat a local radio interview, which begat more gigs, which begat an offer of a deal with an up and coming indie record company, which begat a hit single, which begat another one, and another one.

We did Top of The Pops three times, became regulars on the John Peel show, and even supported the Rolling Stones for one show (John Lee Hooker was ill, and we happened to be the only band in town. But still...).

After the gig, Keith Richards asked if he could play my guitar. When he picked up El Diablo, he looked at me sideways, and then winked knowingly as he played the opening riff to Sympathy for the Devil.

Later, Keith posed for a picture with me. Later still, his dealer introduced me to heroin.

We made it onto the covers of New Musical Express, Melody Maker and Smash Hits.

All through this El Diablo never left my side, and never let me down. She became my trademark, and part of music lore. I made sure she was on every album cover, picture disc and concert poster.

Gibson got to hear of it and offered to give me a real SG, if I agree to get rid of El Diablo. I declined, which sent Alex over the top in a thermonuclear drunken hissy fit.

"Are you fucking mad?" He screamed. "The biggest guitar company in the world have offered to give you one of their guitars, and you'd rather play that cheap piece of shit?" His foot lashed out, kicking El Diablo from her stand

Even though I'd killed two people, Alex Scott was the first and last person that I ever punched. Drawing on a lifetime of experience, I knew exactly where to hit him. The first punch broke his nose, the second his cheekbone, and the third and fourth resulted later in an eye-watering bill for cosmetic dentistry.

That was in the Green Room of The Old Grey Whistle Test, which explains why Alex didn't appear that night.

A week later, a couple of days before Christmas, we played in Belfast.

I hadn't seen Alex since I smacked him. He flew to Belfast on his own, joining us for the sound check before the gig.

I felt nervous at being there. This was the height of The Troubles and you could feel the tension in the venue. But we played a storm, the crowd roared their approval at every song. Halfway through the set, Mick was introducing the band when Alex stalked across the stage, grabbed the microphone and pointed to me.

"And this little shit is our lead guitarist. The IRA blew up his brother, if any of you are in tonight, I'll buy you a drink."

El Diablo buzzed in my hand. Burned behind my eyelids.

Half the crowd cheered, while the other half booed. And then it kicked off. We ducked as a hail of bottles and broken seats clattered onto the stage.

Mick froze. I didn't blame him.

Jimmy came across to me. "We've got to do something," he yelled. "This is like the Stones at fucking Altamont."

I played a familiar riff. Jimmy nodded, patted me on the shoulder, and then looked at Tom.

"Stiff Little Fingers," he shouted.

Tom nodded. Mick looked petrified. "I don't know any," he said.

Jimmy shrugged. "I fucking do."

He stepped forward to his mic, "1-2-3-4...!"

I played the riff again, and the crowd roared as we thundered through a monster version of "Alternative Ulster".

When we finished, the house lights came on and I saw the full extent of the ongoing carnage. The auditorium was a frenzied mass of vicious sectarian fighting. Amid the violence I saw a familiar face battling his way to the exit.

It was our last ever gig.

Backstage was chaos and we got separated in the melee. When we all made it back to the dressing room, Alex was nowhere to be seen. The unspoken assumption was that he'd made his own way to wherever he was going.

Jimmy looked at me. "What he said was out of order. Are you OK?"

I said I was fine.

El Diablo continued buzzing in my hand, and in my mind.

Alex was found three days later. He'd been shot through both knees and the back of the head. His hooded body left next to a burnt-out car on a patch of wasteland in Bandit Country.

The Turtle Doves split up after the Belfast gig, I haven't seen them since.

After that I bummed around. When a solo career didn't work out, I did some session work and got by. And then my mum died of cancer, and I lost interest in everything. I wasted every penny that I earned as my habit took hold, and my life spiraled into a nosedive towards yet another "Live Fast, Die Young" rock and roll cliché.

Looking back, I've forgotten more than I can recall. Can't even remember the last time I played.

I tried to pawn El Diablo the other day. The pawnbroker laughed at me. People can smell desperation, and when you're a fallen rock star and drug addict, the only place you'll find sympathy is in the dictionary, somewhere between shit and syphilis.

Most of my veins have collapsed, I'm half blind (injecting yourself through the eye will do that), my teeth have rotted, and I've got ulcers all over my body. My worldly possessions are this notebook, a pen that I nicked from a betting shop, a sleeping bag and the clothes that are hanging off me.

And that fucking guitar. Immaculate as the day I bought it, while my life has turned to shit.

This morning I woke up under some bushes. At least it didn't rain. One of the newspapers I'm lying on is a couple of days old. The frontpage story is about a British Army patrol killed by the IRA in Londonderry. There are pictures of the victims, one of whom is Shaven-Headed Guy, AKA the late Sergeant Major

Adam Lane, 2nd Battalion, The Parachute Regiment. Best friend of my late brother, and pallbearer at his funeral.

The last time I saw him we were standing over the body of Alex Scott, Adam's Browning 9mm still smoking in my hand. Adam had broken Alex's leg so he couldn't make a run for it – he was good at breaking bones, was Adam – and then told me where to shoot him, to make it look like a hit.

Alex screamed like a baby, said he was sorry for all the times he and his brother beat me up, snot pouring down his face as he begged for mercy. I was high as a kite, but I remember laughing when I blew his kneecaps out, and the stench of him shitting himself when I pushed the gun barrel against the back of his head.

After a lifetime of imagining scenarios of slow, violent revenge, I thought killing the Scott twins would make me feel better. Instead, all my dark fantasies turned into terrifying nightmares - hideous dreams from which I wake screaming. And when I go for too long without a fix, my night terrors return as daylight hallucinations.

The gift that keeps on giving.

When I'm not high or hallucinating I think of Sid the milkman, how it felt to batter his head on the pavement, cracking it open until his brains leaked out.

Lately, I've seen him every day. Sometimes he talks to me, but mostly he stands to one side, smoking a Woodbine, smiling quietly, looking at his watch and biding his time.

I pick up the damp newspaper and read the story about the IRA bomb.

Sid's waving to me now, beckoning me towards him. I stand up and sling El Diablo's strap over my shoulder for one last performance. The railway line's vibrating and I can hear the train a'coming.

"It's a Friday," said Sid. "Everyone pays their bills on Friday."

Rock Star Suicide

Rich Anthony, lead guitarist with the rock band, The Turtle Doves, has been found dead in an apparent suicide. Anthony, 27, of no fixed abode, was hit by an express train at approximately 7am on Christmas Eve. Since leaving The Turtle Doves, Anthony suffered from drug addiction, and mental issues brought on after the recent loss of his mother. A police spokesman said that Anthony's trademark red guitar was found undamaged near the scene

---

Born in England in 1962, Richard grew up in a small market town in rural Herefordshire before joining the Royal Navy. After 22 years in the submarine service and having travelled extensively, Richard now lives and writes in rural Worcestershire.

DIMINISHING
Gabriel Ricard

The office would endure, and the universe probably wouldn't pull off the vintage network TV miracle magic trick of eating its own face. Even so, Graeme needed a prop on his desk to give his sentences, especially the ones damming somebody for something, a sense of completion. He settled for some blank sheets of paper. "I think we're done here," he said, shuffling and then tapping them on the desk a couple of times. In the few seconds of that action at the end of the sentence, he imagined for a second the entire history of people shuffling and tapping papers on their desk, signifying that it was time to move on to the next mildly complicated disaster.

All in all, the musical history of the gesture was a pretty disappointing one. Graeme had already obliterated Marvin Stengel from the office, and he was moving on to his next accomplishment for the day. Accepting that his greatest moment of divine inspiration for the day was going to be that whole thing about what a century and change of papers tapping against a desk would sound like with the ambition of angels starting a choir group in their spare time.

"Come on, goddammit," Marvin rose from the seat only halfway. He still had the skin and hair and eyes of someone who suspected that someone somewhere was finally going to arrest him for everything he ever did as a teenager. "I had a hell of a time getting here, and I—"

"Need the job," Graeme answered for him. "Yeah, we covered that, right before you almost tripped over your own feet, and into my desk." Looking down at his desk, at the papers, at the society that tried to swirl into being within the grain of the wood on the desk was probably making him in turn look stupid. "And I still smell Old Crow whiskey on your breath," he continued, reluctantly giving him the eye contact that would hopefully hustle both back to the logical conclusion this should have met five minutes ago.

For a moment, Marvin was distracted from trying to say everything he had ever wanted to say at a doomed job interview. "Jesus," he said, pumping two short, sharp breaths into his right palm, "You're good."

Graeme stared back at him and felt the beginning of the physical toll that emphasized why playing poker usually gave him a migraine by the end. "How's that?" He tried to will the alarm clock to be more proactive about taking violent measures against people who wouldn't leave his office.

"It is Old Crow," he said. "That's what I drank this morning."

"I'm honored for the insight," he said, wanting to look out the window, picture the sounds of the city moving up towards him one floor at a time, and be forced to remember silence exactly as it would never be again in just a few seconds.

"I brushed my teeth though," Marvin said, quiet and casual with the frayed, carpeted floor all of a sudden. They were friends, the morning after something awful had happened. "I put the rest of her in the freezer, and then I had, well I guess it was three more drinks," he looked up, "But with ice," and he used his index finger to drive this part home.

"You did what?"

"I'm an alcoholic," he said, still looking at him, smiling like someone who had grown to be OK with everyone being disappointed in him. "And I'm getting old, but I can still be a functional drunk." And then he grinned the way people do in doctor's offices. "I take pride myself where I—"

It was selfish to want to make up for almost missing it. "Not that," Graeme said, taking an unexpected interest in how much space two people could fill up in a tuna can office. "The freezer," he said, his hands exhausted and motionless on his desk, "The freezer part."

"Right, when I killed my wife last night." He shrugged, smiled as someone would after scanning their debit card the wrong way at the grocery store. "I told you that like two minutes into this thing."

"You...," He had to either swallow or finish that sentence. "The hell you did."

The difference between the person Marvin had been a few minutes ago, and the person he was now, was the difference between someone who had been auditioning for a play for the past week and had someone who had just finished running the lines for the director. "Look, I'm not gonna freak you out with a whole desperate little fish in troubled times thing." He sighed, the way someone would when contentedness was a welcome runner-up to resignation. "I'm sorry to waste your time." He got up, running his hands down the jacket of his suit as he did so. "It's obvious that I'm not going to get anywhere without making some serious changes, and I gotta say thank you for reminding me of that." He extended a hand. "And thank you for your time."

Graeme noticed that Marvin's fingernails were a little on the long side. He almost groaned lifting his arm up, or rather letting the climate control in the room lift his arm up, in order to shake Marvin's hand. "The freezer," he said, almost whispering.

"Don't worry about it," Marvin said, shaking his hand firmly-but-not-too-aggressively. "It's just one more thing I gotta figure out." He laughed the way people do when they only have a couple of minutes to catch up on the metro. "It's been a really, really weird year."

Graeme stopped his arm from plummeting onto the desk. He instead simply lowered it gently, painfully.

"But it can only get better from here." He turned away. "That's what they say in the meetings," he continued, opening the door to leave. He turned back to Graeme. "Have a great day. Good luck finding somebody."

The door closed. Graeme stared at the door, and lost track of time. When he looked at the clock after a while, the time indicated didn't mean one thing or another. He looked at his phone, thinking about the people one called in these situations, wondering which words were the most rational for explaining what had just happened.

Unfortunately, he suspected his arms were done with stressful exercise for the day.

He couldn't remember a single piece of conversation from the first half of the interview but tried again to recall something anyway.

THE ODDITIES ON SATURDAY NIGHT
Gabriel Ricard

"Want some company?" For a few seconds, Daniel was pretty sure he wasn't even going to ask. The cigarette was just an excuse to get out of the house. Smoking indoors was allowed. It was just that things were a good deal calmer out here. Not better, necessarily, but calmer. There were at least a few ugly stories playing out indoors right now, and some of them had the potential for collateral damage. He saw himself as just too drunk, too tired and too much in the mood to go home, stay home and leave his phone in the freezer, to feel like watching a series of human car crashes jockeying for his attention. Or his participation by association.

He walked towards the car, smoking, even though Adam hadn't given him an answer yet. He wasn't sure what the answer would be. It was easy to guess though. Adam was one of the all-time legendary assholes.

Instead he just shrugged. Something happening on the front lawn was holding most of his attention. "I don't give a shit," he said. "I'm just running to the store."

That almost qualified as a pleasant surprise. "That's fine," he said. "I need to get some cigarettes anyway."

Adam nodded, watched whatever he was watching for a few seconds longer, and then got into the car.

Daniel looked back. A lot of people would call it a compelling scene. From where he stood, he could clearly make out the smoke from the living room fire that no one had decided to deal with yet. A good deal of the party was now congregated outside. No one wanted to miss the floor show. There were a couple of them. One was an excruciatingly dull, remarkably childish fistfight being held on the front lawn. Daniel didn't know the idiots involved, and he could only guess that it might involve the damage to the kitchen, the bedroom upstairs, and the fire in the living room that was slowly making plans to get out of control.

The threesome on the hood of someone's car was almost as boring, but it was commanding an even more dedicated, noisy audience than the fight.

"Are you fucking coming?"

Daniel turned back to the car. "Yeah, shit, sorry." He got into the car. Ten years ago, a ferocious buzz of humanity, insanity, possibility and weirdness expressed with disconcerting casualness would have been fine with him. It would have been impossible to imagine being anywhere else in the world.

"It's the store just a couple of blocks up the way here," Adam said, lighting a cigarette at the first red light. Not a single siren could be heard. Not a single cop car flew past them on its way back over to the house. That was normal. If only the surrounding streets could have been filled with decent people a few generations ago.

"I appreciate it."

Now, a get-together like this, strangers chattering, trying to get laid while dreading Monday, it was just a fair enough excuse to avoid having to stay home.

"Yeah, well, my karma is fucked up," he replied. "I need to do something good before the week is out, and something nice for you better count for double."

Stigmas could go straight to hell, or wherever unrealistic expectations went to enjoy a retirement spread out across eternity. The one Daniel was thinking of was about drinking alone. He didn't think the idea deserved so much negative press. "I didn't know you were a big believer in karma."

"It's a bad habit. I blame it on genetics."

"So, that's why you didn't tell me to go fuck myself?" He thought about getting some beer at the store, too. He was still thinking of how the evening could have just been a two-block trek to and from the apartment. "Or, you know, wait until I got into the car, push me out the passenger side when you get up to 55?"

About a block to the store now. It really was a short drive, but it might be possible to drag the time out a little once there. It was too far a walk back home from where they were now. "You really think I'm that emotionally invested in fucking you up?"

At least it was a gorgeous night. Ridiculously, unrealistically cool for mid-April. Somehow, the fact that it was twenty degrees cooler than usual made Daniel pay more attention to the common surroundings. "I'd hate to think we had all that spectacular history for nothing." He wasn't even sure why something like the temperature would have him staring out the window more than if it was 80 or even 90.

"All bad," Adam said.

"Yeah," he said, trying to give the conversation some personality by laughing when he said that. He looked out the window at the last red light. He could see the store, but he could also see the details of every other building, of the cars around them, of the people walking by and what was going on in one alley or another. Weather like this made him want to put on a thick jacket, head out into the world, and intrude on some of these specifics. Or just pick at them from a safe distance, until they became even smaller, more interesting details.

Instead of the bullshit menu in its current state.

Maybe that was the problem. Maybe it was just a first-world boredom thing.

The car had stopped at the corner. Finding parking around here on a Saturday night, technically a Sunday morning, was usually impossible for any venture. Downtown was a lot like that party. People came out because they were pretty sure it beat staying at home. The liquor store down the street from the movie theater sold candy bars with everything and benefitted from smart marketing when Thursday midnight movies came around. Daniel wondered faintly if finding parking like this meant some good luck was going to hit him in the back of the head sometime soon. It was fun to think anything could happen. This little errand technically qualified as a surprise of sorts.

"So, what the hell brought you to that party?" Adam asked. The question suggested conversation, and it didn't fit the person asking it at all.

No sense in lying to the man. "Boredom," he said. "And I thought I'd see if Lou Ann was gonna be there." No sense in lying, but he had almost kept that part to himself. Lou Ann was just the start of what could potentially be a thousand different things neither one of them should bring up.

He held the door open for Adam to go through first. It seemed like a nice thing to do.

"She's still talking to you, huh?"

It was a big, bright store that would have killed or confused any drunks or junkies that might stagger on through. At this time of the night that was the heart and soul of the clientele. There were a lot of neighborhoods around here that needed a place like this to be on constant standby. It was as good place to walk to at four in the morning. Daniel wasn't sure why Adam had bothered driving. "Not in almost a year," he said. "But she's back from school for a couple of weeks, so I thought I'd try my luck."

Adam was still smoking his cigarette. "I didn't even know she was back." The cigarette got a nice scowl out of the four-hundred-year-old Korean woman working behind the counter, but she didn't say anything. Her lifetime of experience in this store told her it was just better to wait until they were gone. She had her reasons for working in a huge convenience store at this hour. Those reasons were bigger than the two of them combined.

"Someone told me." He shrugged, waited for his eyes to get used to the unwholesome light. "I guess 'what the hell' was the prevailing logic there."

If Adam needed something specific, he wasn't acting like it. His footsteps were slow and made up the only noticeable sound in the entire store. Faint music overhead that didn't really need to be there. "Me too," he said, "As far as going to the party went. I have no idea why I went." He crushed the cigarette on one of the shelves. "I guess even a journeyman malcontent can only take so many nights of drinking alone and watching Netflix." He was scanning the shelves as slowly as he was walking. His face, arms, and legs didn't believe that picking up the pace was going to kill time any faster.

He wanted to ask him if he was going to buy anything, but he wanted to ask the obvious question, the dumbass one. "Did you run into her then?"

"Who? Lou Ann?"

Jesus Christ. Who else? "Well, yeah," he said, "Who else would I be talking about?"

"A lot of people in the world," he replied, turning the corner. "Felt like half of our whole freaking sewing circle was at that house tonight."

That's true. It had likely become even more of a bullying mob scene imposing its will on the rest of the agitated neighborhood. Unless of course, the cops finally showed up. "Fair enough, but, yeah, I meant Lou Ann."

For no discernible reason, he reached out, and knocked several rolls of paper tells off a shelf. He looked back at the Korean woman, but didn't smile, or do anything to try and draw her out. That seemed to suit her fine. She didn't move, glare, or give any particularly outgoing indication that she was even alive.

Daniel could imagine her slipping back and forth the living and the dead on an hourly basis.

"Yeah," Adam finally replied. He turned the rest of the corner and greeted the new aisle with a bizarre little jump and click of his heels. "I saw her for a few seconds, but she was talking to someone else." He grabbed a can of ravioli, threw it in the air, caught it and spiked it on the ground like a football. The sound in a store like that was like a grenade that could also scream, but the can didn't explode from the unexpected attack. "Didn't talk to her though."

Daniel followed him through all of this. Getting those cigarettes and leaving was still important, but it still wasn't urgent. And something going on right now could wake him up. The last thing he wanted to do at home was sleep. "Regrets kicked in, huh?" He wasn't sure why he said that. All kinds of awful doors could now fly open over the next few seconds. "The past comes rising up to bite your feet off, right?"

It wasn't like he didn't know the guy was weird.

"Regrets?"

"You have a few?" God, he thought, almost groaning, no bad jokes at this time of the night, please. "Sorry."

"The threesome you, she and I had would be one." He threw another can on the ground, gave the Korean woman another glance, and frowned a little when she just kept staring at him. "Running you over with that car would be another."

Somehow, in some magic trick that involved forgetting about the obvious, that night, both of those things happening over a twelve-hour period, hadn't even been what he was thinking of a moment ago. "To be fair," he began, "You were only going about ten miles an hour."

He grabbed a bag of peanuts without looking at them and ripped the package wide open. "Getting her pregnant, and then going to Iowa for a month." He emptied the contents into his mouth but didn't chew or swallow. "Leaving her to deal with that by herself," he went on, mouth jammed with food. He spit the peanuts into the air, and then moved just shy of being hit by them, while taking a very low theater bow.

The pregnancy part had occurred to Daniel earlier in the party. Adam had indeed skipped town, and it wound up falling to him to help Lou Ann get through it. The consequences of not wanting to do that, and having the courage to tell her so, was still one of those weekends he only ever thought about at the most inopportune times. Also known as a lot of the nights he stayed in. It was one of his reasons for not even trying to make eye contact her tonight.

As things stood, or at least wobbled along, he had no plans to mention any of this. It was slightly less strenuous to let Adam do the talking.

He looked at the peanuts on the floor and imagined the next person on shift would have to clean them up.

The Korean woman continued to watch them. The way a pothead watched whatever happened to be in their direct line of vision. No real interest, but, you know, it was there, so why not?

"Anything else?" Daniel asked. He watched Adam move a little more quickly down the aisle. He was not the same person he had been in the car a little while ago, but that's the way it went with him. Daniel had honestly not given it much thought at the time. He was remembering now. Adam moved through life like a billionaire's hopelessly disorganized film festival.

Adam had turned the bow into a demented stride that also incorporated knocking things off the shelves at random. "Oh, we could go on and on and on with it," he said. "Fucking miles."

"Yeah." Everyone even remotely attached to their circle loved Adam, despite every awful thing he had ever done.

Certainly, he had been enough for Lou Ann to hopelessly complicate and then destroy their six-month engagement.

In retrospect, polyamory had been a bad idea at that moment in time.

He whirled around, as though his feet really were on a dime. "We should get a fistfight going."

Unpredictable scratched a concrete surface with a toothbrush. What Daniel suddenly wanted to ask about was the night Adam had shown up at that dinner party thing Lou Ann had tossed together. He had come as the friend of a friend, he had to think for a second to remember that it was Harland, but no one else had shown up yet, so it was just himself, Lou Ann and this fucking lunatic dressed for the worst of the summer in the dead of winter.

"You get, like, five seconds to decide," he said. "Or I get to decide."

"Hold on," he said. He wanted to know what Adam might have said to her that night. "What the fuck is even going on here?" He wanted to know what they could have talked about in the fifteen minutes he had left the two of them alone to get drinks.

"Two." Adam stretched his arms and cracked his neck. The hideous light above flickered as though cheering dully.

Fifteen minutes was a long time for someone who could do things like disappear to Iowa, not die, and then come back with five grand in the bank. "Are you trying to get us fucking arrested, man?" What the hell? What the hell?" He wanted to take a step back, but he didn't, unable to trust the world behind him.

"One." He cracked his knuckles on that last number. Then he smiled way too much.

He was great if you didn't have to see him every single day. The dinner party came and went. After everyone had gone home, they had sex in the kitchen while doing the dishes. When the morning cold swooped in to swallow up their apartment's shitty heating, Lou Ann mentioned offhand and under the covers that it might be fun to go out with Adam some night. Daniel remembered agreeing, thinking of how many times Adam had gotten him to laugh at dinner.

Things got out of hand from there.

The five long seconds had come and gone, but he was still standing there, still smiling, and keeping his clenched fists at his sides.

Should have said something to Lou Ann, he thought. Even a polite, painfully strained smile after a hello could have sent his heart soaring, with all the things he could have said or done when they were still together. As it would turn out, neither he nor Lou Ann had intelligence or college education necessary to say no to Adam very often.

The Korean woman probably still didn't care.

"So, you're just going to stand there?" He took a step back. "This is the longest five seconds I've ever experienced; I'm telling you."

And still nothing. The overhead lights buzzed and whirred as though they were doing Adam's thinking for him.

The car ride over here should have been impossible, and therefore unable to happen. Asking him for the ride in the first place should have been impossible, and therefore a faint thought that spoke softly against all the noise on the front line.

But those things weren't impossible and talking to Lou Ann still was.

"Let's just get the hell out of here," Daniel finally said. The OK Corral would have burned itself down, waiting for a showdown this drawn-out. "It's been a long night, and I—"

Why was that the cue? It was a question that was asked as a single rushed out sound. There wasn't a lot of time to ask the question properly. Adam had sent them both crashing into the shelves of various canned foods. He was quick for a guy who qualified as somewhat heavy. Three punches already scored against his ribs, before he even had much of a chance to react to the pain of smashing his back against the shelf and all those cans.

It had been probably fifteen years, maybe even more, since he had been in a real fight. It wasn't like the time before that was filled with an endless parade of brawls though. It used to take a lot of bullying to finally get him to react. Even so, he moved so quickly that he didn't realize he had just smashed Adam in the head with a can of tuna, until he had already done it. Twice. That did the obvious job of dazing him, and he used that to tackle Adam into the other side of the shelves.

Unfortunately, there were only bread products, so it didn't have the same impact.

"This is exactly what the hell I'm talking about!" Adam laughed, just before he gasped at two good punches to the stomach. Bread wasn't the greatest weapon in the world. It wasn't even the best weapon in the store.

Still, Adam grabbed the nearest loaf, and managed to daze Daniel by smashing him in the face with it. He used it a few more times, disfiguring the loaf beyond recognition, and decided it would be a good idea to follow this up by throwing as many loaves at him as possible.

Without a lot of time to really think about whether this was fun, Daniel only had time to hate Adam for stealing his idea, and then react to that. He fought his way through the loaves of bread and hotdog buns colliding with his head. It might have been a good idea to bring a weapon along. Nonetheless he was able to reach out, just as a loaf of honey wheat smashed into the right side of his face and get close enough to catch Adam with a left hook to the side of his head. The gesture needed something to follow it up, so he grabbed Adam by the back of his shirt, the other hand hooked into his pants, and he threw him over the shelf and into the next aisle.

Jesus, he thought, that was kind of impressive, wasn't it?

He moved quickly to get over to the other aisle, but he made it a point to grab as many canned goods as he could carry. Thankfully Adam was just getting to his feet as he came around. All the cans but one missed, and that only struck him in the chest. It wasn't the most ideal of circumstances for offense, but he stepped towards him anyway, and met two pretty good left hooks that came at him in surprisingly rapid succession. They should have brought the old Korean woman's unappreciated floor show to an end, but the adrenaline had apparently and finally kicked in. He wasn't even aware of his heart beating, and his body didn't feel heavy from everything Adam had done. He was living a past life under hypnosis, which meant that all of this only seemed and felt real. He was sitting in a small, air-conditioned office in a huge, blisteringly hot city. Everything was coming out into the open, and someone was taking notes.

"Ever see Alien 3?" Adam asked suddenly. He grabbed the neck of Daniel's shirt as he said this and hurled him face first into a display of 2-liter sodas. "That was my favorite in the series."

Daniel lay amongst the sodas for a second. A little surprising, he thought dimly and gratefully, that those had endured like the ravioli can. He groaned, and rolled into a couple of short, nice, lean kicks to the ribs.

"I think it's because the story they're not telling," Adam said this while grabbing a 2-liter from the floor. "I don't know if that makes any sense, but that's something you're always going to find in my favorite movies." He brought the bottle down as though it were a hammer. "My favorite stories are the ones I can imagine improving somehow." He brought the soda bottle down again. The swing didn't have his full force behind it, but it was still meant to hurt. "Not that it was a bad movie." He threw the soda bottle aside. Doing this was what finally caused it to explode. "I guess I just wish sometimes I could have been a writer, a filmmaker, something like that."

The sound of carbonation fizzing and soda spraying everything it could touch rung slightly in Daniel's ears. It disappeared into the vacuum of sharp pain that followed Adam kicking him again.

"I don't think I could be any of those things now," he went on. "Once you hit thirty, I think it's pretty wise," he paused to reach down, tap into a surprisingly deep reservoir of physical strength and help Daniel up from off the floor. "To just embrace the things that are never gonna happen."

It was strange as an adult to have someone bring him to his feet like that. Not a single thing on Adam so much as suggested someone who could pick up a heavy human being. He had the same tired, nondescript face and body that a lot of people he knew did.

The glass case that was probably there to protect the old Korean woman from robbery barely reacted to having a human being's head driven into it. It would have put him right back down on the floor, but Adam held him up.

"It's not giving learning to fix your own drinks."

He met the old Korean's woman eyes for just a second. Her eyes were still flatly, terminally committed to revealing nothing. He didn't feel like he had a lot of time, so he pushed back on the counter with his feet, using his back for the force needed to send both to the ground.

Not too long ago, he had come to accept the possibility that maybe he and Lou Ann wouldn't have worked out anyway.

He was throwing wild, unprepared punches. Being on top of him helped, but a few punches missed, and hit the hard, filthy linoleum floor. God bless the adrenaline, he thought, but he was still able to know himself to guess at how much more he had in him. At this point, the best of what his ability to handle horrible surprises like this should have left him and then town ages ago. He thought about this as Adam threw him off.

"It's like those guys," Adam said, breathing heavily, "You know, they work in some dumbass office, started playing guitar when they were stupid kids."

His plan had been to get up, take enough steps back to put at least a few feet of distance between them. What happened to this plan was that he fell over just from trying to get up. The best he could do was to grab and throw every candy bar he could get his hands on as Adam dove towards him.

"And then they hit forty, keep playing those shows at Irish Name's Big Irish Pub," he paused to drive an elbow down onto the side of his head, "And actually believe it's 1975, which is probably the last time bands in bars got lucky."

Sparks flickered over his eyes for a second, but they flew ahead to be somewhere else, when he almost blacked out from the second elbow landed on the same spot. Make a fucking point already, he thought, and then went back to the struggle of both staying awake and fighting back. Was this the end of the second wind? The third? It was hard to keep up with that kind of thing. Breathing as though the room was going to do away with oxygen at any moment was something, he hadn't felt in quite a long time.

For some reason, Adam rose quickly and shakily to his feet, instead of continuing with the barrage of elbows. He grabbed a shelf, looked down at Daniel, and grinned like an overeager comic book villain. "You know, Daniel," he said, "We've been through a lot, and I think the reason for that is because I've always, God knows why," labored breaths shook almost every word, "I've always liked you."

The shelf came down. Daniel tried to move out of the way, but it didn't happen quickly enough, and the shelf came down on his back as he was trying to get up. It didn't really hurt. Items fell all around him, and the weight of the shelf itself was a pain in the ass, but he was able to push it off, and then stagger a few steps into another shelf.

"It's not some kind of romantic thing," Adam went on, coming after him, "As far as that goes, I've never seen a long-term thing in—"

Daniel reacted to Adam charging him with a ferocity that surprised himself. He caught him with two good punches to the ribs, one to the side of the head. It had to be someone else's instincts that told him to grab Adam and throw him into one the doors protecting all the priceless 40 oz. malt liquor beverages.

This got a wheezing laugh and cough out of him. "Nonetheless, I've just always sensed in you something of a kindred spirit." He turned. "If that makes any—"

One memory was trying to push through all the others, as well as the small cuts and perspiration on his forehead. He was listening to Adam, but he wasn't giving him a chance to finish his sentences. Every punch was a bigger reminder of how drowsy his arms were. It wasn't even a question of going for any body part. Every single one connected. Adam didn't seem to mind.

When he felt like this burst of enthusiasm was coming to the end of the tunnel, Daniel grabbed him, and shoved him into the next aisle over from the one they had been fighting in before. Adam crashed into a shelf, turned away from Daniel, and stumbled a few steps towards the front counter, clearing another row of items in his daze.

This inexplicably created an outburst of silence. All he could hear was a faint buzzing, and the argument between his rapid heartbeat and languished breathing.

Then the sound of the little bell ringing as the door opened. It was a bunch of high school kids. Drunk, stoned, or desperate to pretend they were both.

"Tell you what." Adam rose slowly and held onto the left side of his ribs. "Let's see this through to the end."

Daniel was already ignoring the high school kids. They had no idea what they were in for next year. "Okay."

"If you win, I don't know, whatever you want." He was taking deep, deep breaths, trying to work some oxygen into whatever was hurting him the most.

He remembered the last time Lou Ann had kissed him. It was a very good five seconds worth of her tendency to hate distance or quiet. He could remember looking at the kitchen counter right before she did, because he didn't know what to say to her after that weekend, when Adam had skipped town.

"I win, we get in the car, go to Memphis, and find something to do."

The high school kids might have been watching all of this. They might not have been. He really wasn't paying attention to them. Or the Korean woman. "Memphis," he said. He was already planning what he was going to do next. "What the hell is in Memphis?"

Gabriel Ricard writes, edits, and occasionally acts. He writes a monthly column called Captain Canada's Movie Rodeo at Drunk Monkeys, as well as a monthly called Make the Case with Cultured Vultures. His 2015 poetry collection Clouds of Hungry Dogs is available from Kleft Jaw Press, while his 2017 novel Bondage Night is available through Moran Press. Recent releases include A Ludicrous Split (Alien Buddha Press/Split chapbook with Kevin Ridgeway) and Love and Quarters (Moran Press).

He is also a writer and performer with Belligerent Prom Queen Productions, currently working on a follow-up to their 2016 immersive theater show Starman Homecoming. His movie podcast Cinema Hounds, co-hosted with an actual man from Florida named Chris Bryant, is currently in its second season.

Despite having never run into legendary actor John Astin during one of his many trips to Baltimore, Gabriel currently lives on Long Island with his wife, three crazed ferrets, and an inability to stop ordering delivery.

A Dark Thread

Justin Bog

Late May

Lindsay detoured off the main hiking channel between Bear Valley Mountain and Ice Creek, part of the western upper Cascade Mountain Range, took the less popular but still scenic cut-off trail to Eagle Lake. She hiked with a backpack filled with printout sheets from the State Parks Department (even though she didn't need them—an old salt) and a compass. Because of the wetter-than-usual spring, the trail remained muddy with standing water in mountain-bike ruts. Her hiking boots stuck with the muck and Lindsay didn't mind at all. She'd spray off her boots when she got home and rinse her car mats. A little dirt never hurt. The mosquitoes, on the other hand, would be swarming soon enough. Today, the chill in the air dampened their numbers.

This particular trail soothed her empty-home-life thoughts, and she'd hiked it dozens of times over the past twenty years, mostly alone, since she couldn't find many other people who loved the trail to Eagle Lake as much as she did. One of her hiking acquaintances told her she felt a weird vibe—a spooky intuition jolting her mindset—about the place. Lindsay scoffed and avoided talk about New Age belief systems. The parking area was almost empty, the main hiking loop being the most popular near her small town of Cross Mountain, but the cut-off trail was considered a difficult hike and could take up to four hours, the reason most people avoided the trail (some were just tired of sharing a trail with bicyclists and there were a few of these people who

wanted to start a petition to ban them from the trail—
and an equally vociferous bunch opposing them—
Lindsay kept silent when talking politics, left that for her
husband).

Lindsay loved the challenge on the path to Eagle
Lake. It was her favorite and one of the most scenic to
explore—weird vibe, my ass, Lindsay thought. She
would even venture off trail as the brambles lessened to
search out places where she imagined she was the only
person ever to set foot there—she took photos for her
hiking blog—and searched out off-trail spots to hide in
for her search-and-rescue dog training course. Lindsay
wanted to be able to train canines to search for lost
hikers. She backtracked in practice, retraced her steps
in known woods, gave false trails, and hid so that the
dogs in the program could find her. They all did, the
scent of a human most striking in any wilderness. It got
her heartbeat elevated and she always burned calories.
This morning, dog-less, she slowed her pace a bit,
enjoying the first spring jaunt. She carried a full water
supply and a brown bag lunch, a couple of energy bars.

Douglas fir, cedar, maple, and pine trees, large
budding ferns, bordered the path, competed for
sunlight. Lindsay was a backyard biologist who loved
spring run-off, the wildflowers peeking out from the
carpeted floor of salvia and other mossy ground
coverage. She knew most of their names and lead tours
for other nature lovers when the Parks and Recreation
department needed volunteers.

Today, though, was reserved for her, alone. She'd
wanted to take a new acquaintance, Jane, out. She'd
been pestering Lindsay to do just that. For some reason
or another, Lindsay delayed Jane. She found Jane
needy, wanted something to fill an unknown emptiness.
Jane was apt to include her son, Noah, on some of their
hikes, and asked if it would be okay, and, although

Lindsay thought Noah was a good teen (*so unlike my own son when he was that age*) she couldn't tell Jane she preferred the company of adults—it would be too rude. Lindsay didn't encourage Jane but somehow her friend was wearing her down. A new friend wouldn't kill her, she thought. Sharing was easy for Lindsay and Jane was nice enough, a woman who wanted to befriend Lindsay so quickly—maybe that was the reason she felt so easily compromised. Lindsay had an ingrained reservation to immediate intimacy.

The spring wildflowers sprouted, peeking out of the ground, the bulbs and early huckleberries, the chattering of smaller animals hunting, killing and eating their prey, the calm in the wild and the variety found in this natural habitat soothed and made her feel small, grateful. The few early-season outdoor enthusiasts who passed by, most of them saying a toothy hello to Lindsay on this sunny day in May, felt the same way, got it deep down in their bones. Lindsay knew some of them too. In this area of the Pacific Northwest, Cross Mountain was relatively close to the foothill town of Concrete and the larger city of Sedro-Woolley, a real bedroom community far enough away from I-5 and Seattle to make Lindsay feel the hectic pace of the next generation was but a curiosity that should be placed under a glass dome on a mantel above a roaring fire. The town's population grew because of its idyllic mountain setting, but most teens trapped in Cross Mountain thought it was a dead-end ruin.

* * *

The shadow of a cloud passed over Eagle Lake.

Spring arrived here in full force. Grasses grew longer on the shore side. The sheer, near-impenetrable cliffs encircling the lake stood sentry. Few braved the circuitous route beyond the wall. Rock climbers came and went from time to time, took photos and posted them on Facebook for all to see. "Look at me way up high, a speck in the sky," but in May they were nowhere to be found. Most who came to sit on the shore side of Eagle Lake relished the journey, the hike up to the idyllic spot through mostly old-growth forest, but these adrenaline junkies seldom returned there. Something unspeakable haunted their thoughts, and this dreadful memory quickly faded when they climbed back into their cars at the trailhead. No one could pinpoint exactly what was bothersome about the place. Those with this insidiously changing mindset would never find Eagle Lake postcard perfect upon reflection, but Lindsay kept coming back, the defensive aura around the lake ineffective. These few hikers ignored the little voice within telling them never to return.

The lake remained calm, the surface a mirror.

In the depths a different shadow awakened—a trigger pulled, like pulled threads, the right amount broken by a hiker's oblivious walk through a meadow riddled with them, a set trap. It had been patient over the decades, waiting. It felt a tug, a connection made—the image of Lindsay in shadow, approaching the mossy bed in a dark glen, a former miner's shanty, coalesced. It had been asleep for so long. The changes within and without finally completed it waited for this moment of reawakening—the threads called. The chilly water temperature had never bothered the shadowy form. In the darkness of the lakebed it had slept.

It reached out, testing its abilities, the body supple and strong, the arms thin and wiry. The cold didn't penetrate. It swam up from the depths, one sure stroke at a time. Water creatures scurried away, a primordial fear response, tadpoles and fish darting away. A male beaver on the far side of the lake shuddered within his twig lodge as the shadow passed far below, heading for shore. When the beaver's mate swam back into the nest and found her equally frightened partner, they abandoned their home and Eagle Lake as quickly as possible.

Sunlight burned into the shadow's features. It winced as it rose from below the water. Concentric circles spread across the lake's surface. All at once it rushed out of the water, splashing in a frenzy until it reached dry land and ran for the cover of darkness within the tree line. It knew exactly what ground to cover and it was swift.

* * *

The Eagle Lake hiking trail widened, once a road leading prospectors into the mountains to mine, which made the hiking easier until it hit steep switchbacks all the way to the large, deep, comma-shaped lake. An avalanche of rocks surrounded the dark water three-quarters around.

Lindsay never felt the need to climb the far steep side to gaze beyond. She imagined more mountain peaks over the horizon, planting her own personal achievement discovery flag. It was too far to go solo, taking paths less traveled, leading into darkening woods. In her backpack among the energy bars and her compass Lindsay loaded pepper spray. Not just in case she ran into a bear (they leave you alone if you leave them alone) but in case a man, or men, fixated on her, teased her. She was a woman hiking alone and she was worldly wise enough to know she could be a target for the wrong kind of person. She'd had one scary confrontation over ten years in the past now, only one, when three men coming up behind her at the beginning of a hiking trail spoke loudly, crudely, purposefully, about Lindsay in nasty ways, had laughed at how she wanted it from them and described how they could give it to her. Lindsay stopped walking and waited for them to pass her. They liked what they saw, thought it was harmless talk: No, go ahead of us. We love the view. Lindsay turned, jogged back to her car, rushed in, and locked the door. The catcalls and laughter of the three men rang in her ears for a long time and she could recall that sound, drag it out whenever she felt tension. She didn't want frat-like men, toxic boys, to ruin her enjoyment of hiking, and Lindsay loved to hike alone.

Lindsay allowed her mind to wander as she herself wandered up the trail. Her husband moved them away from the cluttered streets north of Seattle. Her friends calling Cross Mountain "The Boonies," a more than two-hour drive from the Space Needle, twenty years ago. Before that, they spent almost ten years rooted in the military dirt of Everett. Lindsay wasn't happy there, too much civilization for her, box stores, strip malls, driving back and forth. They had ten-year-old Stephen Jr., and Lindsay wanted him to grow up loving the outdoors. Everett's environment consisted of paved concrete, detour signs, highway congestion, and the usual travel frustrations common to most large cities.

So, they moved to a rural town, where home prices weren't as inflated, where Stephen Sr. could work at a local military recruitment office. Stephen Jr. could begin sixth grade, junior high, at the Cross Mountain Middle School, and they didn't look back. Stephen Sr. said time and again it was the right move. Lindsay loved the mountains, the air so different from the Everett sprawl. She did miss the water, the Puget Sound, so close there, but it was only a little over an hour's drive to the water from Cross Mountain, where the small artsy towns sold waterfront tourism. You can't eat the view, her mother always said. Cross Mountain was a less expensive place to live. Property was cheaper twenty years ago and during the debilitating housing disaster, they hadn't lost too much value. They weren't selling anyway, but if they needed to sell, they'd come out okay. Lindsay and Stephen Sr. remained happy, comfortable with their lives, their life together.

Lindsay couldn't believe two decades passed like a blink. Time felt distorted, magical. Stephen Jr. now worked across the country in New York City, one of the lucky few newly hired who kept a job at the stock exchange after the worst of the economic meltdown.

"But, Mom," Stephen Jr. crowed, "I'm doing amazingly well, better than great, since our boss made the right call all along!"—Stephen Jr. spoke of his boss as if he were a god to be worshipped and Lindsay always tried to extinguish the puffery.

"Yes, Stevie, that's nice, and your father will love to hear it, but I'm off for the afternoon Parks and Rec meeting." Lindsay, well aware of his penchant for protecting her, anyone really, from harsher truths, knew Stephen Jr. didn't always tell her everything. He was so used to putting a shiny gloss on anything troubling. Lindsay also knew Stephen Jr. was low man on the totem pole at his investment firm, worked long hours, longer weeks. He only told her the positive side, a shield against imagined negative consequences.

Stephen Jr. returned home for Christmas if he had a fiancé to show off, which had only happened twice (a college fling and two Christmases ago), both times Stephen Jr. saying: Isn't she amazing? Lindsay and Stephen Sr. nodded and kept their opinions to themselves. It was nice seeing Stephen Jr. as much as they did, which wasn't often what with life busy being NYCity life. Stephen Jr. would call and when Lindsay mentioned the current woman he'd grown infatuated with, and that's always the way Lindsay pictured her son's relationships with women: as infatuations, he'd say he'd moved on, the search for a mate taking up less and less of his time, if it happens it happens, but I'm not looking for true love again. Lindsay wished he'd keep all this to himself; he'd always been an intrepid approval seeker—another needy soul.

Lindsay said nothing since she knew Stephen Jr. as only a mother of an only child could know her own son. A perfectionist, he took after his father, and, along with being a perfectionist, Stephen Jr. had that puppy dog quality no woman could stand for too long. He wanted to make her so happy, wanted to spend time with her, wanted to know where she was every second of every achingly long day, always texting, always leaving cell messages, too many love notes—someone breaking it off, someone inevitably saying: You care too much. Hashtag smothering.

Lindsay would never tell her son he suffocated her too. When Stephen Jr. chose Duke because his grandfather filled his head with tales of southern charm. Her father, now two years in his own Anacortes, Washington, grave resting beside Lindsay's mother. Her father died from heart failure after taking care of his wife over her final years of dementia. Lindsay grieved still. Even in his college choice Stephen Jr. tried to make someone else happy, and Duke accepted him, great grades and the usual community outreach programs after school. Lindsay almost jumped up that very second to help him pack upon hearing the fabulous news that her son would become a future Duke graduate.

Stephen Jr. had never been away from home for any extended period and he whined about how much he'd miss his mother (never saying how much he'd miss his father—keeping it real—what will I do without you?) right up to the moment they said goodbye that first college year at the Bellingham airport. Enjoy North Carolina. Duke is an incredible place. Try to make new friends, she added, sounding a bit weary. Lindsay didn't say what she really wanted to say: try to grow up without me.

Stephen Jr., two days ago, spoke passionately about spending time as a member of the Brooklyn rowing club.

"You're part of a big team and no one can slag off, let the team down. Wow . . . it's energizing, Mom, you would love it too, out on the water, all the buildings rising up around you like you're in the middle of a pop-up book." He told Lindsay he'd been hanging out with his workmates at the clubs until all hours of the morning celebrating his thirtieth birthday. She and Stephen Sr. couldn't fly to join the party.

Lindsay often pondered the life of Stephen Jr. on her long hikes. She couldn't help it. She worried about him fitting in and he did fit in according to all the cheery news, but she wondered what he'd do if she showed up and surprised him. Would he be drinking alone in a dimly lighted, sweetly rancid-smelling, corner bar with the regulars? His desperate façade-o'happiness a symptom of a nebulous want he couldn't define. Lindsay shook her head, clearing her thoughts, and felt nature calling. She had a little time, and all her off-trail exploring proved useful, up ahead was the perfect spot, a secluded decades old miner shanty, the planks of wood walls rotted away, the square of the long gone domicile still apparent, the dirt floor covered now with moss, trees grown up, nature once more hiding man's hovel.

When the urge to relieve herself grew, Lindsay stepped off the hiking trail and made a quick path through the pine tree branches on autopilot, needle-less where the sun couldn't reach. She followed a slight opening between the trees and the shade from the towering branches lowered the temperature to a light chill. Now she felt like an explorer and wondered when the last human had stepped off the trail to walk this particular area of the woods. What had happened to the miner who built the shanty she headed towards? She felt just as untethered, rebellious, wanting so much more. It was so daring, forging a path no one had walked before.

I am Lindsay, Pacific Adventurer!

The image, conjured up, made her bark out a laugh. Pith helmet, mosquito netting hanging down in front of her eyes, the roar of wilder and much more vicious animals filled her imagined primal forest. Lindsay must've walked a quarter mile through the trees with spring buds sprouting, the carpeted ground growth still low and easy to walk across. She didn't worry about getting lost. She found private spots each time she hiked. Men were so lucky they could just whip it out against a tree and pee like dogs. She'd been to this un-mapped cave shanty several times before—and thought of it as her own private outhouse.

Lindsay walked out of the tree line and onto a gently sloping meadow, mounds of wildflowers dotting the field, the wildflowers like threads of color. She moved through these mounds of threads, broke them, and squished them beneath her hiking boots. She spotted the dark shanty, a natural cave with dappled sunlight unable to intrude much. It was possibly an abandoned mine entrance, barely excavated at one time, the rock too unyielding to continue man's hubris. She made sure there weren't any nettles and stepped into a mossy area made blacker green by the largest cedars Lindsay thought she'd seen in the Cascades so far this spring.

A strange—

(funny)

—white lining marked the moss, bordering the edges, clumping, pasty in spots—the shape of a body outlined in chalk, just half an outline. She had too active an imagination, loved true crime shows. Lindsay's scientific nature made note of it. She'd never seen it here before and there was a lot of it in the clearing. In the shadows, the white moss—*Is it a fungus*—stood out like lace doilies on a heavily varnished dining table.

The urge to pee took over and Lindsay pulled her backpack off and laid it on the moss, the straps covering the chalky white. For every animal or plant a parasitic invasion to fend off or live with in symbiosis. Even the human body had its cohabitants, microbial, helpful when left alone.

Lindsay drew toilet paper from her pack, unzipped, crouched down and studied the ground around her for a second. After finishing, she dug a shallow hole, tearing a bit of the moss, and placed her biodegradable wastepaper in and filled the hole with loose dirt, broken moss pieces and leaves. Then, she took her pocketsize camera (the one huge extravagance her husband loved spoiling her with this past Christmas, her Fuji—no iPhone camera suited her thinking—old school) out of her jeans and took a close-up photo of the white—she'd have to call it a fungus of some kind. She took one photo, checked, and then turned on the flash feature. The next shot came out perfect, capturing the pretty way the white laced the edges of the moss.

There, a single pink threading, caught Lindsay's attention. She placed her camera an inch above the pink thread-like offshoot and made sure the photo captured the fungal mass with every one of its vibrant pixels. She didn't see the pink thread move; she was too busy focusing the camera lens. When Lindsay looked at the photo screen the pink was gone, as if the thread had never been there or dug its way deeper somehow.

Lindsay looked for it. She poked into the white moss with her finger. Strange. Bewildering nature.

Stumped, Lindsay's backyard biologist's curiosity blossomed. There were so many species real biologists knew nothing about. The worst of nature often hid its true intentions behind beauty. Lindsay remained wary of anything she didn't understand and that's why she loved doing research. It was the sheer stupidity of man that nature always showed up.

She felt something (a spark—her heartbeat increased) was watching her, a prickly awareness rising. Her intuition spiked in alarm and she twisted to see behind her, out the opening between the tree limbs. Nothing was there. It looked darker outside the glen. She heard a shuffling and froze in place. She was in an awkward position, her torso turned. Get on with it.

Lindsay watched—Oh God—as a dark man-shaped shadow closed in, a racing engine of spiny limbs, and she fell backwards a step—

Stop scaring yourself, Linds.

Crouching, Lindsay would only remember how she lost her balance standing so close bent over with her camera. She fell. Not hard at all but enough to make her laugh, sticking out her hand to stop her fall. Soft moss-covered ground ideal if you're going to fall on anything. Being left-handed didn't help Lindsay maintain reliable poise; Stephen Sr. and Jr. shook their heads at how many times Lindsay had fallen, tripped through doorways, taken a wrong turn. She collapsed on her side, her face resting inches above the moss, right at the edge, her cheek lowering softly against the white edge, her lips parting with a startled, audible grunt in the stillness of the forest. She didn't see the pink thread, thinner than a single strand of hair, as it darted between her lips. Lindsay didn't feel or taste it.

The entryway darkened once more and she watched the shadow and dim light play, a spinning top. But *I saw a man, a shadow.* Her thoughts spiraled away, out and back, a kaleidoscopic dance she tried to still.

Lindsay thought she heard a snapping twig as if someone—*something*—was walking outside the dark glen, but there wasn't anyone there. The field beyond the glen remained empty. Her vision darkened, and filled up with blackness, then to a pinprick. She turned her neck and tried to roll over on the mossy ground. She hadn't fallen, the shadow, this darkness engulfing her, placed her on the mossy bed, it activated the thread. Lindsay's mind was not her own in that instant.

The darkness took her.

* * *

Four hours later Lindsay awoke. She remembered falling, *fainting*, but nothing more. The shanty filled with a blacker darkness as the sun declined and she could barely see five feet in front of her. She stood up, the muscles in her legs twitching, tight. She needed to stretch but fell back onto the mossy ground. She imagined leaving the natural cave with the sun now beyond the mountain peak. She needed to get home. She brushed cobwebs and dead leaves off her jacket. She needed water. Her mouth felt so dry, but the thought of drinking water made her feel ill. No dog had found her, this lost woman.

Get up scatterbrained child! Can't even make it to Eagle Lake.

This is how Lindsay scolded herself—get moving. She'd fallen asleep. I've never needed to nap, what a crock, she thought to herself, then: I'm getting so old.

Later that evening, when she'd eventually tell her husband about her clumsy fall, the moss-stains on her new hiking khakis, he'd barely find the energy to say, be careful; he'd been saying the same thing almost weekly, monthly (What is it about southpaws? He laughed with Lindsay when he dated her so many years ago; he found her tripping and stumbling—you're my beautiful klutz— endearing back in their courtship days). Driving home, her thoughts darkened. She viewed the decades of his constant joking about her clumsiness as sexist, a subtle gaslighting. He wanted to keep her in her place: let a man take care of you. She shook this thought away.

Tonight he'd then, as if she'd been keeping him from more important matters, turn all of his attention to the day's news, keep watching Fox for the first report before switching to MSNBC for a chance to catch up on the other side's faulty insistence—*can't they see?* Lindsay would join him soon after she put together a salad, rubbed salt and pepper into chicken breasts with a little olive oil and cajole him into getting out of his chair just a moment to get the gas grill going out on the back deck.

"But I'm watching the news, the real news, not that fake kind? It started already. I wasn't the one who was late getting home today."

Lindsay pictured how her evening would go and she grew cold. Lying there in the middle of the forest on a patch of moss-covered earth (the softest mattress couldn't compare) she felt that her husband should make his own dinner tonight. She stretched down there on the green soft ground beneath the tall trees of what used to be a man-made shelter, the moss once a dirt floor swept with a pioneering woman's broom, letting her thoughts take her further and further into the past. Once more concentrating on how her son may as well live in another country, and then thinking that as far as she was concerned her husband, who lived under the same roof, also lived in another country. We've always appeared so in sync though. That thought slivering in made Lindsay think of angels on her shoulder pointing out the obvious.

Stephen Sr. would come home after work and need to restore energy. He hated the commute, still more than half an hour to Burlington, where the recruitment office had moved, bigger and larger forces at work. Stephen Sr. spoke to local high schools, community colleges, and made a presence at the outlet mall, assigned canvassing draws, and held parent hands. Numbers still wouldn't change much, and the spark of joy sucked right out of him. Work was a chore, no fun anymore, day after day. Lindsay would not be the cause of this joylessness.

Only today, at this very moment in the shelter, she believed Stephen blamed Lindsay for this, that he would become more and more angry with her, and her thoughts went to the next logical

Illogical—thirty years of married bliss— remember.

step: would he ever become physical with his anger? He'd taken on a lot of the rage swirling around the political landscape and made it part of his nightly diatribe. Lindsay would listen and listen and listen and never argue—some of it, her husband's viewpoint, she stridently believed as well, but people have to get along. They were a military family and they followed a certain military and political philosophy. In thirty years of marriage he'd never hit her. He despised violence, crimes against women especially.

Cut their balls off!

Stephen's exact statement when he heard about anything done to any woman by some stupid meathead raging redneck or rich shit hiding behind his lawyers, but Lindsay now, that niggling, wriggling tension entering her mind, thought this was a legitimate possibility. Ridiculous thoughts. She scolded herself for leaping from A to Z when the thought of her husband becoming abusive, physically threatening to her, had never crossed her mind the whole of her marriage. She knew other couples couldn't say the same thing and counted herself lucky. She'd caught a good man, but, wow, now, she failed to erase the image of her husband backhanding her across the face. It would pop up now and then until she found herself at home, startled by the grass stains on her khakis. She'd been gone hours longer than she'd planned. The time flew by. She'd try to remember lying there in the dark mossy glen—sleeping.

What rubbish . . . get up and get going.

Lindsay indulged herself in fantasy thinking. Stephen Sr. wouldn't hurt *Me*—he took spiders outside when she found them in the dark corners of the kitchen or bathroom. He was a recovering Catholic, almost ready to forgive the church for all of the huge, disturbing sex cover-ups, but Lindsay knew he'd forgive the church and he'd be back in the pew on the major holidays.

Stephen never frightened her before, not even a prank, jump-scaring her from behind a doorway. He seldom raised his voice either, and Lindsay could only remember the ten, twelve times in thirty years where they'd argued so loudly the disagreement dissolved into both of them laughing at the fact that something so little could cause them to behave so badly towards each other—and usually it wasn't what they were arguing about, any subject, but rather the tone of voice the words were spoken. They saw other couples in public going at each other tooth and nail, the nagging, the putdowns, the undermining passive aggressiveness on full peacock display, and they rolled their eyes so happy they never treated each other that way. Lindsay liked to argue without rising anger adding anything to what should be a civil debate. She hoped Stephen Sr. could remain that way, sharing peaceful intentions, his easy going way, her way too, she really did, since Lindsay now began to believe otherwise.

Don't be ridiculous.

Lindsay finally stood from her bed of moss, the light faltering, weaker with the sun's position hours ahead of where Lindsay thought it should be. How long had she lain there wasting time thinking about her annoying son and her secretive husband? He was keeping a big secret from her. Lindsay convinced herself of this. She put her backpack in place. She hadn't eaten her packed lunch, but she wasn't hungry. She needed to get home. She left the glen and hiked up the small meadow, entered the pine tree forest and covered the short distance through the trees to the hiking trail. She brushed a cobweb off her face and wondered what her husband's face would look like when he was really angry with her. The contorted features, his dark blue eyes blazing in the flickering of his precious television light and Lindsay began to form a plan that would mean never having to see, or fear, her husband ever again.

This is madness. I don't fear my husband.

By the time she arrived home, planned a simple thirty-minute meal of beans and rice, fajita-spiced flank steak, the thread, so fine a filament, had taken firm root—in the next few days the thread would branch off—duplicating. Lindsay's thoughts, oppositional and unnatural, shocked her even more.

Early June

Once again, Lindsay worked on dinner before Stephen Sr. arrived home from work—why did he even need to go into the office on the weekend? Pondering this while stirring the stew-like butternut squash and roast chicken minestrone, simmering so the bottom wouldn't burn, she waited until the last minute to put everything together.

Stephen Sr. liked to unwind in front of the television, drink a beer or two before eating. She made an arugula salad dressed with lemon zest and olive oil, added herbed croutons, sunflower seeds, and organic cucumber wedges cut into half-moons. Her knife work in the kitchen swift and sure, Lindsay sliced a Walla Walla onion into semicircles and added them to the salad bowl. The edge of the sharp knife fascinated her, and she caught herself staring at this edge . . . a minute passing.

Stop it!

Her minestrone grew thicker after adding small wheat *gemelli* pasta (*gemelli*, the Italian name for twins, dual personalities, named after a psychologist, which made Lindsay laugh when someone had told her this at one of her husband's military parties—trivia being king at a social gathering—has your husband ever been stationed in Italy? It's an amazing place to earn a living off Uncle Sam—wink, wink) not really a twin at all, but a single strand of s-shaped pasta twisted to make it appear as two coiling links, snakes—maybe conjoined twins—was one of her husband's favorites.

Stephen Sr. lumbered into the kitchen, placed his briefcase on the kitchen work desk in the corner, and pulled a Kirkland Amber Ale out of the refrigerator. He glanced at her, stopped, said, "You're hiking too much, getting too skinny."

Lindsay kept her distance, said, "Hi, Honey, I'll eat two bowls of minestrone. I made your favorite with lots of spice." Somehow, Lindsay spoke without breaking her smile. She wanted to—

Keep the peace.

Yes, keep the peace with her husband. She knew this would take all her willpower after the disastrous afternoon spent in the company of her new friend, Jane, who was now at the top of her short list of old friends she never wanted to see again. She replayed the afternoon in her mind and was convinced Jane was someone Lindsay could never confide in. Jane was fake, someone who talked about wanting to learn how to garden but didn't own a gardening implement to begin digging in the dirt.

Lindsay rubbed her hands on her apron (*I am thinner, fit, stronger, forget him, fuck him*). Through the window over the kitchen sink she watched the wind blow the flowers and tree limbs lining the backyard fence, wild yellow roses, swirling and thorny blackberry bushes, and foxglove, fuchsia dangling, all to form a wall of color in the spring and summer. A bit of wild mixed with the formal. If only they had a Pacific madrona tree, so common nearer to shore, majestic and protected with pale trunk and peeling reddish bark. They couldn't afford a water view, so they didn't live that close to it, and remained land-locked in their subdivision miles on the wrong side of I-5. Cross Mountain. How did they ever end up in this overly quaint town? Lindsay felt her mind wandering so quickly from topic to topic she barely heard her husband's response.

Stephen Sr. didn't walk over to give Lindsay a kiss as he usually did, he'd been avoiding her these past few days, giving her space. He looked spent, and Lindsay wondered how sitting behind an army-issue desk could tire him out so much. What else was he up to? It was a Saturday and still it bothered Lindsay, his departure every weekend. When would he say enough is enough?

Her husband escaped the kitchen, and Lindsay wanted to follow him into the television room to ask where he really went that afternoon, every afternoon. She would watch for his telltale expression, raising his eyebrows, showing the whites of his eyes a bit too much, the puzzle lines on his forehead crinkling. He kept his gray hair military short and his ears stuck out a bit too much, something Lindsay had always loved about him, her own Jughead Jarhead. Her thoughts spiraled and Lindsay sunk into them.

A second later, this nickname made Lindsay cringe since they humbled his otherwise too handsome, too available, flirty, appearance—a joke shouted out by her husband's best friend, Milton, Milty, at one of their backyard barbecues, when they thought none of *the wives* were listening, equating a married man to a hockey goalie. Laugh. Laugh.

Just because your husband is a goalie doesn't mean I can't still score!

Women flirted with married men all the time. She knew this was Milty's defense. Wear the ring and it didn't stop some of them. He was living proof of that; Milty loved it, loved flirtatious, easy women. That's how he'd met Candy. She started flirting with him at a military bar. She had her eye on him the minute he'd entered the place with Stephen Sr., and he had allowed her bubbly personality to latch onto him. She'd been with an equally flirtatious bobble-head, but her charms didn't work on Stephen Sr. and she pouted away at Candy's obvious success with Milty. Lindsay thought Milty was a pig and he'd never given her a reason not to think of him this way. Lindsay once said to Milty: Why are men incapable of getting mad cow's disease? She waited a beat for Milty to answer before saying: Because they're all PIGS!

Milty, being thrice divorced with another girlfriend, Candy, The Determined Bar Cruiser of four months, pressing for her own ring, said, isn't she a beauty, when introducing Candy to them over drinks at Chili's one Friday night (as if Candy was a bright shiny red sports car). Milty had custody of his two teenagers, after his first wife walked away (she hated the military life but faked it good for four years—*that's fer sure*, Milty said as his mind filled with disgust). His second wife was also on the rebound, too young, couldn't handle the children and walked away inside of two years, promising to keep in touch, but Milty hadn't spoken to her in over six years. His third wife lasted the longest but also ended up walking away, having found a richer, handsomer (not possible, Milty said, chagrined) civilian lover without kid baggage. She wanted her own and got them.

Still, he was quite a catch, Lindsay thought, and must be doing something right and something very wrong—enough to cajole three women into saying, "I Do." Lindsay thought his two kids were the best part of Milty, but that was then; now Lindsay believed the kids brought nothing but trouble, not unlike the way her Stephen Sr. viewed Stephen Jr.

Candy was about ten years younger than Milty, and wanted her own baby, but also wanted the ring to cement her place. Milty didn't want any more kids and Lindsay knew it too. Candy would lose that battle as the last wife did. She told Milty without a ring the future stepchildren would get confused about what role she's playing: Mother or Not a Mother. Lindsay wanted to tell Candy that Milty's two teenagers would never think of Candy as the mothering type.

Lindsay filled with humor, wicked; she had her own thoughts on what role Candy was playing but kept them to herself. Milty was handsome, a true military piece of rock, still solid with a windblown masculinity after almost thirty years work abroad and on the base with Stephen Sr. She once imagined what Milty was like in bed, all his aggressive, lusty strength transparent, while Stephen Sr. kept all his masculine prowess locked away when in the bedroom, strong, but vanilla through and through. Stephen Sr. was a big softy and had let his body go a bit doughy around the middle. He's still a head-turner and that's what you love about him, Lindsay thought, defensively, realizing she was having an internal debate with herself. Stephen Sr. and Milty, and whomever Milty was shacking up with that year, spent a lot of their off hours at Lindsay's home. Again, Lindsay didn't want to go out to eat all the time. Even with a military pension looming in the near future, she didn't think the economy was done riding a constant coaster. Happy Hours were okay once in a blue moon but even then, Stephen Sr. had to joust with Milty for the bill, as if paying for the entire tab made him more of a man. Lindsay wanted to scream.

She resisted the impulse.

Stephen flipped channels constantly (*God he was such an irritant*) stopping on a rerun of a talking head's show from Friday and Lindsay wished he'd just turn a blind eye to all the nonsense (Stephen Sr., not the talking head—who was cagey enough to know what side of the bread to butter) and enjoy the quiet spring evening, the hummingbirds flying up to the red-dye-sugar feeder hanging from the eve outside, centered in the kitchen window above the sink. The wind blew insistently, rising for one last spring storm before the dry season started. The foxglove tips dipped in the wind and this movement focused Lindsay's attention on another beautiful but deadly species, so many holding the balance of life and death, made her think about going outside one last time.

No no no never again no more walking hiking I can't do it and you can't make me.

She heard Stephen Sr. change channels with a click of the remote, a quick silence broken when the ad for a top MSNBC show buzzed throughout the lower floor of the house. Lindsay wondered where this pundit had come from, since it was like she'd suddenly appeared fully formed, Venus on the spouting-head half shell, rising in persistence, mongering a different kind of fear, oppositional to the others on Fox who had captured her husband's full attention for years now.

If Lindsay could line them all up against a graffiti-strewn wall, light cigarettes, give them each a few last words (Oil Money, Worst Person In The World, Birth Certificate, Grim Reaper, Epic Proportions, Huge, blame the old Tea Party liars, Deficit, Gaming The System, Tell Momma I Love Her, Shutdown, Cruz Control Stuck, Lipstick On A Pig, Bigly, I don't know her, No Collusion) before signaling the firing squad to shoot on the countdown from three:

3

2

ONE!

Lindsay would welcome the quiet.

She didn't talk politics with Jane earlier that afternoon. Didn't even know if she was right or left. This didn't bother her as much as she thought it would. Her husband walked back into the kitchen for another beer. He moved slowly, his guilty demeanor blaring, and placed his empty into the recycling bin.

We have a great marriage. He wouldn't throw it all away like Milty: *"4th time's the charm! Ain't Candy a looker?"* Lindsay wouldn't be able to boost her courage enough to actually spit out an accusation. She wasn't raised that way. She'd sweep the ugliness of life away—she thought in the next instant of dirt floors, the shanty floor, the darkness, sweeping dust away, burying something there—Lindsay could picture a skeleton, ancient, buried there beneath the moss, and a thread, searching.

She shook her head, thoughts pinging now, but Lindsay couldn't shake the image of Stephen Sr. in the arms of someone like Milty's Candy. Her long French-manicured nails highlighting soft fingertips rubbing his jug ears as she murmured into them how she knew what to do to drive men like him wild.

"The soup smells terrific," Stephen Sr. said, startling Lindsay out of her thoughts, "as always." She frowned.

Lindsay stirred the pot with a wooden spoon. The minestrone had been simmering for two hours and she didn't want it to start sticking to the bottom, burning. This simple thought returning calmed her buzzing mind.

"Thanks. We'll eat in half an hour." She lost the frown, but Stephen Sr. had to have noticed how clipped her words had become of late.

Stop it, Lindsay. Stop it!

"Fine by me."

"I'm thinking about calling Stephen Jr. tonight—after dinner. He's up late on Saturday nights."

"Suit yourself," Stephen Sr. said before leaving the kitchen. I will, Lindsay thought.

I can do it one last time.

Then, she opened the back-kitchen door, no hesitation, quick as a switchblade, before she could stop herself. She ran past the patio table and chairs, noticed Jane had forgotten to bring in the sugar bowl from their afternoon tea, the one she said she'd get—

Damn her!

—pulled the foxglove up by the roots and returned to the kitchen in a fervent rush. Within her caged mind, she giddily yelled out '*Safe!*' like an umpire. By the time she'd closed the door behind her, each breath she took was ragged, her pulse rapid, blood pressure rising.

The foxglove hadn't grown to its full height. It formed fairy cap blooms, all huddled next to one another at the top. Lindsay chopped the blooms off and threw the long stem and roots away in the kitchen garbage.

She took half the flowering blooms and put them in the smallest of the three Cuisinart food processor chopping bowls, pulsed them into a fine herb scatter, and added this final ingredient to her summer minestrone—steeping.

I know this is wrong sorry wrong and bad, but he deserves it.

The soup simmered and thickened.

Lindsay took out a serving tray. She filled a large bowl with minestrone, dotting the surface of the soup with extra virgin olive oil and grated Parmesan cheese to complete her Italian recipe. She cut two hefty slices of rustic potato bread, again, organic, no high fructose corn syrup in her kitchen, healthy, and finally sprinkled a little hot sauce on top the way Stephen Sr. liked it. The soup smelled spicy, rich, and hearty.

In a smaller bowl, Lindsay portioned out a bit of the salad she prepared earlier and set this in the right corner of the tray, added another beer to complete Stephen Sr.'s dinner and carried the dinner tray into the television room.

"What's this?"

"You had such a long day. Me too, by the way. Jane really wore me out. Don't think she's the right person to join me on my hikes. Thought I'd serve you dinner in here. I'm not feeling quite myself. Sorry if I haven't been myself."

Stephen Sr. didn't like surprises and he was always overbearingly suspicious—she blamed Milty for this too, such a cad. It was a good thing Lindsay had never given her husband reason to be suspicious of her.

All these years of towing the line brought her boundless good to keep doubt at bay. She wasn't a convincing liar; her voice was a little higher than normal, tight, nervous. Getting out a believable apology almost cracked her mousy purposeful demeanor.

Her husband gave in, and said, "Thank you. This is very nice of you, Linds. We don't always have to eat at the dining table, but we won't make this a new habit."

Just eat the goddamn soup and die you bothersome pig of a man!

Lindsay almost laughed out of fear for herself. What was she doing, why was she thinking these— *insane*—thoughts? Not just thinking either, actually doing something, something insane.

"No worries. I think I'm going to go take a long bath. Maybe I'll feel better. There's something going around town."

Stephen Sr. took a spoonful of soup and made theatrical, pleasurable eating grunts. "Whoa. This is some of your best."

"You always say that."

"Because it's true. I hope you feel better."

"I'll clear the dishes later."

Stephen Sr. ate and went back to his political programs. He finished the soup, then the salad, and drank most of his third beer. He contemplated getting up during the next commercial break to refill his bowl. He heard Lindsay turn the bathwater off.

The digitalis worked its way through Stephen Sr.'s system rapidly and within twenty minutes a mild headache intruded, buzzing in the background. He turned the volume down. Not soon after that he began to sweat, which made him wonder if the peppers in the soup had been the hotter kind. Ten minutes later he stumbled out of his chair, dizzy, head now pounding. He began to feel nauseous, the room swirled, and he barely made it to the downstairs bathroom in time. Maybe Lindsay had food poisoning from testing the soup, and was upstairs, also not feeling well. Bad chicken?

He could hear a callous pundit raging against a Hollywood celebrity who thought the sole reason for his theatrical existence on this green earth, and as an Oscar-winning actor, was to insert himself into the latest hotspot, clean up the debacle. What a putz, Stephen Sr. thought, before vomiting into the toilet. Blood mixed with the soup remains, something strongly acidic and smelly. He collapsed onto his knees, head hanging in the bowl, and flushed the mess away. The pain in his stomach felt like a probing ball of needles, punctures, piercing. His heartbeat raced, his pulse increasing. The pain ripped through every nerve and Stephen Sr. felt delirious with the struggle to even breathe.

"Lindsay!" Stephen yelled once. He didn't realize he had less than an hour of life left, and his system crashed in full distress, battle stations failing.

Lindsay heard her husband retching downstairs—had he called out her name? She tuned the bathroom XM radio to NPR. This was more her speed, meant to comfort. Maybe the soothing soft jazz would make her less anxious.

She turned up the volume, more news at the top of the hour, and didn't hear Stephen Sr. anymore, even when he fell prostrate onto the bathroom area's oval shag rug, placed in the center of the cold bathroom tile. Finally, unconscious, adrift, pulse weakening, Stephen Sr.'s heart finally stopped beating forty minutes later.

She wasn't worried about her husband anymore or even what would happen to her if (and when) someone found out about it. I'm alone. I'm myself now for the first time since before Stephen Sr. Then she made further plans.

Lindsay dressed in old jeans and threw on a gardening shirt with patches on the elbows, heavy socks, and her hiking boots. These clothes now hung so loosely on her skinnier frame—when did all the weight just disappear? Even with the drastic weight loss, Lindsay felt strong, so much stronger. Lindsay searched for one of her smaller belts to cinch in the jeans so they wouldn't fall off her bony hips and rolled up her sleeves. Then, all dressed up for the big chore ahead, she walked downstairs to check on Stephen Sr. He was dead on the bathroom floor, a dark tile and grout that hid the dirt. Goop, offal, and blood, bits of soup, rancid beer, pooled near his open mouth. She took the Lysol and sprayed, covering the close space. She'd rather smell the disinfectant than the decaying ooze and shit.

Lindsay walked into the television room and punched the off button. *Good riddance!* The house became as silent as a tomb, and this thought made Lindsay giggle like a little girl caught pulling wings off flies, burning anthills with a magnifying glass. She had to gather a larger sense of calm against the rising tide of blackness inside her head.

She went out to the attached garage, pulled ten extra-large garbage bags out of the Hefty box, and took the duct tape off the storage shelf in the far corner. She used all the bags, lifting one part of Stephen Sr.'s corpse at a time, sliding the bag underneath and around, duct-taping everywhere. She went back for more bags and ended up closing him up three times until he looked like a big black cocoon. It took all her strength. Lindsay rested, but laughed. All of her true crime-show experts were so wrong. Corpses weren't heavy at all. Lindsay studied her skinny twig-like limbs. She didn't have biceps, but she didn't have loose skin either.

The new Pacific Adventurer Fitness Regime works.

She walked into her kitchen and poured the minestrone down the InSinkerator, ground up all the bits and pieces. She gathered the rest of the foxglove buds into a baggie and put this inside the flour canister on top of her refrigerator, where the other storage canisters, sugar, brown sugar, confectioner's sugar, joined the other pantry staples. One never knew when it would come in handy once more.

After she scoured the counters, floor, and appliances spotless, Lindsay sat at the kitchen desk and dialed Stephen Jr.'s cell.

Pick up pick up pick up you lazy fuck.

It was almost one in the morning in New York City and she got her son's voice mail. Beep: "Stephen, it's Mom. I really need to speak to you (and this sounded off even to her, so she backtracked)—I mean, I was thinking of you and had the funniest memory. You're probably out having a great time at the club you told me about, and I do hate spoiling whatever you have planned. Life is tough sometimes. I need you to call me back . . ."

"Mom?" Stephen Jr. connected with the call just in time, "Sorry about that. It's very late here. I heard the last bit."

"Are you at home?"

"Mom. I was sound asleep. Your call woke me up," and he sounded pissy, and prissy, and whiny, and Lindsay stopped from yelling back at him by sheer force of will—breathe.

"I'm calling to tell you something hard."

"I thought you just said you had a dream?"

"No. I was thinking of something from your past, and, and . . ."

"What is it Mom?" Stephen asked, coming more fully awake, trying now to show less aggravation.

Lindsay's new directive thought coalesced, and she said, "Your father has had a heart attack. You need to come home right away."

There was silence on the line. Lindsay couldn't help thinking: That makes you speechless you little runt.

"What? When?"

"Earlier today. They think he'll wake up from all the drugs tomorrow morning. He may need valve replacement surgery."

"But you're calling me from home. Is Dad going to be okay? He's still at the hospital?"

"I've been with him all day and he's stabilizing but the doctors aren't sure about what to do. It was a mild heart attack, but there's damage to the muscle. They think he needs an operation. You know your father. When he wakes up, he'll check himself out and come home to think about it some more. I came home to change, clean up. Get some things together. I'm heading right back to Cross Mountain Hospital." She rambled, her story getting too wide. "Call the airlines now and get home as fast as you can."

"Okay, okay. I have to do some rearranging tomorrow, today, this morning. It's a Sunday and the office is closed. Why didn't you call me earlier in the day?"

"Stephen, there wasn't time. I wasn't thinking right," (*and that's the only thing that's truthful here*) "and this isn't the time to talk to me about your work. I know that's so much more important to you than your own family, but I'm putting my foot down. Your Dad needs you. I need you. For once stop your whining."

"Mom . . . Jesus."

"Sorry. I'm so sorry. Please forgive me. So stressed."

"Can you pick me up from the airport?"

"No." The thought of leaving the house shocked Lindsay. "No."

"Why not?"

"I'm going to stay by your father's side. You take the bus or cab it home. Fly into Bellingham, a cab or Uber won't be as much from there, but it will still cost a lot. Or rent a car. You make enough money now to afford any of these things, but if you take a cab home, I'll leave fare on the hall table for you. You know where the spare key is if I'm at the hospital." Lindsay knew her son was cheaper than her dearly departed husband, and would take a cab, and use the money she left for it.

"Shouldn't I just go to the hospital?"

"No!"

"Mom, calm down, everything's going to be all right. Dad's going to pull through this. He's young. He's not even sixty yet."

"Call me. There's a slim chance we'll be home. Call me first when you land, and I'll tell you where we are."

"Okay."

"Besides. If I need anything from the house you can bring it with you in dad's car, and I'll probably need something else."

"I can't believe this. Dad's not that old." Now Stephen Jr. repeated his own thoughts and Lindsay smiled because she wanted his guard down.

"I know. He takes such good care of himself." She pretended to cry, let out a longer sigh.

"Jesus. I'll be there by tomorrow evening."

"Text me when you know more about your flight time. And Stephen, please, we'll pay your travel expenses. I don't want you to dip into your savings." That would get him to come home without another complaint. He wouldn't have to shell out his own blue-chip cash.

Stephen Jr. stayed silent. She imagined him thinking: Mom sounds really strung out. I'd feel the same if my longtime spouse just had a heart attack?

If he had a longtime spouse . . .

"Your Dad loves you very much. You know that."

Again, Stephen didn't reply right away. Maybe that line felt like too much embellishment. The word love came out more like a curse.

"I said I'm coming home didn't I?"

"It will make your Dad heal quicker once he wakes up." This made Lindsay stifle a giggle. She knew what laid in store for Stephen Sr.

"See you tomorrow, Mom."

"Travel safe. Love you."

"Bye." Stephen Jr. disconnected.

Lindsay smiled. Her story had so many convoluted holes, but she didn't think Stephen Jr. would even worry his way through them. What if he called the hospital? There's only the one, but, no, he worked on autopilot. As a child he wouldn't think of ever coloring outside the lines, perfect, perfection counts, a lesson he did learn from having a strict military father. Follow orders. Obey one last time.

She dragged—so easily—Stephen Sr. to the open door of the basement and shoved him through the doorway and watched the big black pupae—that's what it is now—bungle down the wooden steps, cartwheeling, the bagging and duct tape so thick and secure nothing ripped. This was an old house from the seventies and most of the basement remained unfinished, half of it still dirt floor, the other half turned into a rec area and man cave. Stephen Sr. and Milty poured the cement themselves over three weekends in the usable space but left the dirt floor in the dark half meant for storage. They finished a big, nasty job, hard labor, but it was nothing tough for these military men—their pride made them insufferable for weeks afterwards. They put Home Depot carpeting down over the cement and added a couple loungers with built-in beer holders, a dartboard, and a foosball table. After all that work, they seldom used it, preferred the front porch or the first-floor television room, and gave it over to Stephen Jr. and his other high school loner types.

Lindsay pulled back the flimsy folding accordion doors they'd installed to separate the remodeled section from the old, dirty, cobwebbed part that remained unfinished. Stephen Sr.'s corpse was heavy, but Lindsay didn't struggle to move him inch by inch. She didn't sweat anymore.

She pulled Stephen Sr. into the dark room and rolled him the ten feet across the dirt to rest against the far wall. A mountain bicycle Stephen Jr. used as a teenager leaned against a wall, both chunky tires flat. Dust gathered on the seat and handlebars. She'd get Stephen Jr. to help her dig a hole. He'd be up for that, surely. No, strike that: she could never get him to do any kind of physical labor. He'd feign a headache, homework, or the occasional asthma attack wheeze. She'd have to do it all herself, and that's the way she liked it. But he'd help her build a new wall after he changed.

Lindsay had known the next part would be tricky: a union of sorts between her own operating system and Stephen Sr. His final use. Before zipping the last black bag over her dead husband's head, she'd bent close to his gaping maw and didn't even feel a tug as a pinkish thread darted from her searching tongue to burrow into the corpse.

She closed the door to the storage area. After turning off the light, she locked the basement door with a key she'd carry with her from that moment on. Safer to not have anyone open it and fall right down the stairs. Shame if that were to happen.

There was more work to be done and Lindsay felt energized in her new world without a husband. But oh, he would change, for the better, Lindsay thought, finally.

She took a hot bucket of soapy water and other cleaning supplies into the bathroom and scoured the toilet, the vile spattered walls, medicine cabinet, floor, and bathtub, the pipes leading down from the sink, everything, until she was satisfied. Bleach works best, something she always heard on those CSI shows. Bleach is my friend, hides the evidence. Then she cleaned the entire bathroom again, top to bottom. What else did she have to do? She used the third mop bucket of suds to clean the floors leading from the bathroom to the basement door. Her calf muscles tightened from the exertion, but not in a bad way. Lindsay felt glorious, as if she'd hiked the longest trail, miles and miles, top of the highest Cascade mountain, and had finally returned.

Lindsay turned off all the first-floor lights and went upstairs to take a shower. She didn't recognize herself in the mirror hanging above her sink in the master bathroom. Her expression stayed serious, pinched skin around her green eyes, tightening, her dark brown hair wet and slick. She could see her cheekbones and then couldn't remember the last time she'd eaten anything.

After putting on lounge wear, more of a caftan with pockets for tissues and scribbled to-do lists, Lindsay felt refreshed and happy. She was on track. She'd get things done in her new world. Jane, and anyone else who called, would find the answering machine with a message detailing how there had been a family emergency and they had to fly back to Minnesota to be with Lindsay's beloved Aunt Celia, but Lindsay wasn't worried about Jane anymore. She would change too. She thought about the shadowed glen in the middle of the forest. The darkness. What was it? Who was it? There was something there that day, something helped Lindsay, as Lindsay helped Jane, earlier, when they said goodbye to each other, hugging, the tip of Lindsay's tongue darting out, touching Jane's neck with a little pink thread. Then, Eagle Lake, a photo memory of the large comma-shaped expanse of water and a ripple across the surface on a windless day. Something beneath the waters stirred. She didn't know if this was a past memory . . . and a future memory, the concept, made her laugh, and it was a horrible laugh, low, rumbling from her shrinking gut.

Others would meet the same happy coincidence—the surface of the water breaking. Lindsay thought about the people in her life, then Stephen Sr. and Jr., both on a distinct path, and . . .

Milty needed to be taken care of too, and Candy, who would receive nothing more ever again except their fate; certainly, no more check-jousting at Chili's, Applebee's, or that waistline-spreading, We-Are-Family, pasta carbonara, fanfuckingtastico Italian franchise. Milty really had been Stephen Sr.'s best friend, remained on the edge of polite, and never uttered much more to Lindsay than the civil greetings and the communal laughter of a man who didn't find her attractive enough to make a pass at.

She'd phone Stephen Sr.'s office and tell them about a death in the family, ask them to use all of his sick leave and vacation time, cancel the newspaper, alert their nosy neighbors, call the rescue dog people and the Parks and Rec brigade to tell them she needed to be placed on hiatus, pull the shades tight, and never use a light at night again after Sunday. With their cars in the garage, as far as the world would know, Lindsay and

Stephen Sr. left Cross Mountain and were vacationing and wouldn't be home for a very long time. Summer in Minnesota. Yes, a humid mess of a place to spend the summer but Aunt Celia needs us.

She was forgetting something important. Milty was part of it, but she couldn't remember what. This new Lindsay felt so good. Her mind stayed so active—always formulating plans, her thoughts a maze. She rested on her bed, ran a palm across the empty space where Stephen Sr. had slept. He was a traitor. Milty too; surely, he was the one who had initiated Stephen Sr. in his adulterous ways. Stephen Sr. joining Milty on one more fishing and crabbing trip out on the Sound, winking at each other, both secretive, slyly catting (guiltlessly) around. She was sure of it. Milty and Stevie out on the town. Wives and mistresses dismissed, abandoned or left to fall asleep alone on their side of the king bed. He deserved his fate. Milty deserved worse. Candy did too. At least Stephen Sr. would rise to a different purpose. *Junior will build a nice wall, shut me in with his father so that I can become . . . and then protect me.*

Forget about Milty and Candy and concentrate on Stephen Jr. That's what had her mind racing. She must be perfect. He must understand. Who says you can't come home again?

Justin Bog, a member of ITW: International Thriller Writers, lives in the Pacific Northwest with his long coat German Shepherds, Eiko and Kipling, and two cats, Eartha Kitt'n and Ajax.

IEP
Agnes Bookbinder

We're here because I'm stupid.

Mom tells me I'm not stupid, but she has to say that--she's my Mom. Everyone else here knows I'm stupid.

Mr. Jones knows.

Miss Perry knows.

Mrs. O'Connell knows.

Even the people I don't know can tell. Our lawyer knows I'm dumb as dirt. He costs $375 an hour, Dad told me, so he's a really good lawyer. He's smart enough to figure out I'm an idiot without even meeting me before today--he just needed to see my report cards and stuff.

Dad knows, too. He knows I'm not worth $375 an hour. I hope he can get his money's worth.

They all know. Only Mom tells me I'm not stupid, but she doesn't mean it. I guess she's a good Mom.

We sit at three tables squeezed together in this tiny room I've never been in before. The tables feel like plastic but look like wood. We introduce ourselves.

Mr. Jones. Principal.

Miss Perry, Language Arts and Math teacher (she also says she's my Special Education teacher, because I can't be in classes with the normal kids).

Mrs. O'Connell, Science teacher.

A lady I don't know, Mrs. Kim. She's from the school district.

The school lawyer lady's name is Mrs. Curtis.

Our lawyer's name is Mr. Michael.

Dad.

Mom.

When it's my turn, I mumble, "Josh."

I'm not sure what I'm supposed to call myself. All the other people have jobs. I don't know what my job is.

"Kid."

There are half-laughs around the table. Maybe I was supposed to call myself something else. I feel even more stupid calling myself a kid because I'm 13. Kid sounds like something a grown-up would want me to say, but then they laughed at me. I don't know what I was supposed to say.

A sheet of paper gets passed around for everyone to sign.

"We're not agreeing to anything. I'm not signing anything," Dad barks. It bounces off the walls.

It's a small room with uncomfortable chairs. The door is closed, and it's hot in here. I can feel the sweat trying to stink up my armpits because I had PE today. Good thing I put on deodorant this morning. Dad's voice sounds a lot louder in here than it does when he's shouting at home. I guess at home, with more space, he's not as scary. He's scary at home, but not as scary as this. Here, Dad's--what was that word from that story we had to read in class today? Terrifying.

Here, Dad is terrifying.

The school lawyer lady tells Dad we are signing to say we are at the meeting, but it doesn't mean we agree to anything. Our lawyer nods. Dad grumbles, but he will sign. Mom signs because Dad did.

Lawyers don't sign, the school lawyer lady explains to Mom when Mom tries to pass her the paper and pen. The school lawyer lady avoids looking at Dad, who is scowling at her. He looks like he wants to punch her in the face. Mom stares down at the table and nods.

"Mrs. MacKay, could you please pass the pen and sign-in sheet to Josh?" Miss Perry asks.

I am sitting next to Mom. She tried to pass the pen and paper to the school lawyer lady around me, but now, she passes it to me with a little shove without looking.

I figure out which line I'm supposed to sign on the piece of paper because there's only one space left to sign, and it has my name on it. The school lawyer lady points there to show me that's the right line anyway. I already know I'm stupid--I don't need her to remind me. I sign and put the pen down. She smiles at me. It's quick and hard. She slides the sheet of paper and pen from me and back to Miss Perry.

The meeting starts. The lawyers click their pens open like starting guns.

"Thank you all for coming to Josh's annual IEP meeting. Thank you for coming this year, Josh. And it's great you could both make it today--," Miss Perry begins, smiling at Mom.

"What's that supposed to mean?" Dad snarls at her. "I couldn't come before because I was working."

"I just meant, I'm glad you could make it today." Miss Perry's face turns red and her voice wobbles. "I know how hard--"

"No, you don't," Dad interrupts. My teachers don't know, but my Dad lost his job. The fastest way to get on his bad side, besides being me, is to make him think about what happened with his job. "And don't pretend you do. What are you going to do to fix what you've been doing with *him*?"

He jerks his head in my direction.

"Josh has been making progress, Mr. MacKay. He works hard."

"Then why can't he read?"

Miss Perry, still red in the face, sighs. "He is learning to read."

"Yeah, but he can't read, can he? You say he's working hard, but it's not hard enough, is it? Either he's lazy, or you all don't teach him right. Or it's both. We should have gotten on this earlier."

I catch him look over at Mom. She's in for it later, and that's not fair. It's not her fault I'm stupid.

"Mr. MacKay," Mr. Jones says to Dad from the other end of the table, "your son has a learning disability. It's going to be hard sometimes, but Josh is a good kid. And these ladies are good at what they do--"

Mr. Jones is way bigger than Dad, but he's always calm. I wonder if he has any kids. Coming from Mr. Jones, a learning disability sounds like it's not that big a deal, but Dad starts clenching his jaw. That means he's pissed. I think it's because Mr. Jones is black. Or maybe it's because he's nice.

"So what do they do that's so great? He tells me he's in a class with 20 other kids. Isn't all of his stuff supposed to be--*individualized*?"

Dad looks over at the lawyer to check if he used the right word. The lawyer gives him another little nod. Right word.

"You can't teach him if he's with 20 other kids. He told me *she* doesn't even teach him--some other lady pulls him out of class to a table in the hallway, and she's not even a real teacher."

Mom looks up from the table for a minute, looks over at Miss Perry, and stares at the table again.

"Mrs. Ramirez is a paraeducator, and I supervise her," Miss Perry says in a louder, more steady voice than she was using before. This sounds more like the Miss Perry from class who tells us to quit fooling around. "She's a professional."

"Mrs. *Ramirez* doesn't have a teaching degree." At home, Dad asked me if Mrs. Ramirez speaks English. I told him she can speak Spanish, too, but she speaks

English fine and she's nice. He told Mom I wouldn't know if Mrs. Ramirez speaks English right or not.

"No, but she's experienced and very good at her j--"

"This program isn't good enough for him. It's not working. He can't read."

"The MacKay's want to place Josh in another school since the program here does not adequately meet his educational needs." Our lawyer finally talks. We've been here for less than an hour, so he needed to do something to get his $375.

"Yeah, and the school district should pay for it, too, because the law says you're supposed to teach him and you're not teaching him. We can't afford private school, so you should make it right. We should have done this a long time ago." Dad looks at Mom again, and she frowns more at the table.

I look up at the clock.

4:00.

We've only been in here for 10 minutes.

It feels like all of the air has left the room, and I don't think my deodorant is working anymore because my armpits feel sticky. I want to go home, but I know when we go home, it'll be worse there. The car ride, too.

The school lawyer lady looks up from the pad where she was writing notes.

"Are there data that show the program here isn't working?" She looks over at Miss Perry.

Miss Perry shakes her head.

"No. Josh met the goals we all came up with last year--all of them. Reading. Writing. Math. He met all of his goals. We're very proud of you for all of the progress you've made, Josh."

I want to disappear into this uncomfortable chair. It was really nice of Miss Perry to say that, though.

I guess it's not just moms who say nice things that aren't true.

Dad starts clenching his jaw again. He looked like he was relaxing a little when he was shouting at all of them, but when they started talking back, the muscles in his jaw started doing that strange jumping thing they do.

"Well, he could have done more. Those goals didn't push him enough. He needs pushed."

"The goals last year were developed by the full team, including parent input, and addressed the areas of his most recent evaluation?" the school lawyer lady asks Miss Perry, who says yes.

Dad glares at Mom.

"And the goals were met?"

Miss Perry says yes again. "He's a Level G in Reading. His calculation and writing are both improving, too."

"The school team can adjust what they're doing, but it sounds like it's working, so you wouldn't want to adjust it too much. If Joshua is making progress, then the program is appropriate," the school lawyer lady says to our lawyer.

"No, it's not!" Dad explodes. His voice ricochets off the plastic on the cabinets on the wall. "He still can't read. How's he going to catch up? You all aren't doing your job."

"May we have a moment? About 10 minutes?" our lawyer asks.

Mr. Jones, Miss Perry, Mrs. O'Connell, Mrs. Kim, and the school lady lawyer all stand up to go. There's not much space between the chairs and the walls and the table in this little room. Mr. Jones struggles the most to get to the door. He winds his way in and out of chairs, and I wonder if he plays football. It reminds me of trying not to get tackled.

Once they all escape the table, they walk past Dad and out into the hallway, closing the door behind them. The blinds on the door tap the window when the door closes--I don't know why I noticed the sound, but I did.

"What the hell are we paying you for?" Dad shouts as soon as the door shuts. "Why am I doing all the talking? $375 an hour, you should be talking!"

Our lawyer takes a deep breath and his tie moves up and down on his shirt. Dad wears a suit and tie today for the meeting, too, even though nowadays, most days, he wears his same college tee shirt for four days in a row. Our lawyer's tie looks more expensive than Dad's tie. I wonder how much his tie costs. Maybe it's $375. It looks very fancy--it's shiny red on his light blue shirt.

"I wanted to explain what is happening and what will happen next. Do you *all* want to stay for this? Does anyone need to use the bathroom or take a break?" He looks at me.

Our lawyer wants me to leave the room. I don't know if I'm allowed to take break. This stuff is serious.

"Ashley, take him out in the hall or something," Dad tells Mom. I guess I'm allowed to take a break.

Mom and I work our way around the chairs and out the door. Dad starts yelling again before we get the door all the way closed.

None of the teachers are out in the hallway. I don't see Mr. Jones or the school lawyer lady, either. I'm not sure where they went. Mom looks at me for the first time since we went in the conference room.

"You okay?"

"I'm not a kid anymore, Mom. I'm okay. Don't worry."

"You know, we had to bring you this year, for this meeting. They invited you, and we had to bring you. But you get to help make your plan. You get to help decide what you're going to work on. And I hope you know that I know you've been working really hard." She pauses and the space between her eyebrow's wrinkles. "They're not usually like this, these meetings. It's your Dad's first year, too. He could never go before--you know, because he was working--so it's a big change."

Mom works, too. She's worked since before I went to school, before anyone figured out, I was stupid. She was working at the same time Dad was, but she still went to all the meetings. Now, she works two jobs since Dad lost his job. One job is at the ice cream place, which is good because of free ice cream. I'm not sure about the other place--they sell pillows and scented candles and girly stuff like that, so it seems kind of boring.

I bet when it was just Mom at the meetings, they didn't have to take breaks. I would have made more progress because they would have pushed me more if Dad came to the meetings, but I can tell Miss Perry likes Mom. I can't read, but there probably wasn't any screaming.

Mr. Jones wanders back into the hallway. He must have been in the office, right around the corner from the conference room. Dad is still in the conference room, yelling at our lawyer. Mr. Jones smiles at Mom and me, and we smile back. He always looks calm and friendly. He's a good principal.

"Can I get either of you all anything? Water, or I think I saw some snacks in the lounge earlier? This is probably a long day for you, Josh."

"I'm okay," I shrug. I'm glad he's not mad because Dad is yelling.

"No, thank you, Mr. Jones," Mom tells him. "But thank you for asking."

Mr. Jones nods. We stand there and wait together, quietly. The school lawyer lady shows up--then, Miss Perry and Mrs. O'Connell--then Mrs. Kim, who is talking on her phone. Mrs. O'Connell is eating a bar with a silver wrapper. I'm hungry. I wish I could tell Mr. Jones that, but we must stand and wait. The silver wrapper is noisy--it crinkles.

The school lawyer lady taps on the door.

Inside the door, the yelling stops.

The door swings open and the blinds clank.

Dad's eyes are different when we all come back in the room. He is still sitting at the table, and he stares at Mom. His jaw isn't clenching anymore, but he doesn't look relaxed. Even though he's staring at Mom, I think he's staring through her.

We all find our chairs again. Mr. Jones and the teachers and the school lawyer lady squeeze their way back into the room. The school lawyer lady clicks her pen to get ready to take notes again. Mom and I sit near Dad. I sneak a look at Mom, who is quiet and staring at the table again.

Our lawyer sits back down next to Dad and begins talking.

"The MacKay's feel that this program is inadequate--"

I wonder why our lawyer says the MacKay's when he only talked to Dad.

"They do not disagree with the evaluation the district has conducted, but they believe that the district has failed to provide Josh with a program that will allow him to access a free and appropriate public education. The MacKay's are interested in pursuing due process and will be filing their letter with the district and with the Office of the Superintendent of Public Instruction by the end of the week."

He used a lot of words that make no sense. He must be a good lawyer.

The school lawyer lady is looking up from her notepad. "The MacKay's aren't interested in mediation?"

"No, I'm not interested in mediation," Dad growls again. He only talks in growls and shouts these days. "You had your chance. And this jerk tells me, with me paying him $375 an hour, that these letters won't do a damn thing."

"Mr. MacK--," our lawyer says with a serious face, but Dad interrupts him.

"Shut up. Shut up. If you're not going to do anything about this, then we no longer need your services."

My teachers, Mr. Jones, and the lawyers look surprised with how Dad is talking now. I can see their faces out of the corners of my eyes. Mom and I stare at the table because we know how he can be.

Mr. Jones speaks first, calmly. "Mr. MacKay, I understand that you're angry, but the district has a civility policy. That means --"

"I have a civility policy, too."

Dad has a smile in his voice, which is calmer now. He takes his gun out from under his suit jacket and sets it on the table with a tap. Mrs. O'Connell gasps, and it feels like any air that was still in the room just got sucked into her lungs.

The quiet in here is worse than the screaming. I can see a teardrop slide down Mom's nose and onto the table. She knows not to make a sound. I wish I could give her a tissue.

"You, wh--, that's a gun--I--". Our lawyer sounds like Miss Perry did at the beginning of the meeting. My voice cracks like that sometimes because of puberty. His tie is moving up and down faster on his shirt.

Dad is still smiling. "Yeah, it is. I have a concealed carry permit for that, and this is an open carry state. It was rubbing. I feel more comfortable now."

"Sir," Mr. Jones says, frowning, "this school is a gun-free zone. You should go."

"No, that's where you're wrong. I don't have to go anywhere. You can't throw me away like I'm garbage and think that you can do whatever you want with my kid, stick him somewhere and forget about him. If I don't do my job, I get fired. *This* guy," he jerks his head at our lawyer, "doesn't do his job, he gets fired. How come you think you get to keep your jobs when you're a bunch of incompetents?"

"And I have rights. I think if you ask these lawyers what all the legal stuff is about gun-free schools, they'll tell you that I can have this gun in this school. I have the permits. I know my Second Amendment rights. As long as I'm not using it to intimidate you--and I'm not, I took it out for my comfort--then I can have my gun here."

The school lawyer lady is staring hard at her notepad when she tells Dad, "Revised Code 9.41.280 says that you may keep your firearm locked in your car while you are here on school business or may have it in your car when you are dropping off or picking up your son. You should go."

I look over at Dad for the first time in a while, and his jaw muscles are dancing but otherwise, he doesn't move. He doesn't say anything. I don't think he knew about 94.142 or whatever the lady said.

I look around a little.

Mom's head is pointing down at the table. There's a puddle of drops on the table under her nose now.

Mr. Jones stares at Dad with a serious face.

Miss Perry keeps her eyes on the paperwork in front of her like she's reading it. I pretend to read a lot when I'm not really reading, so I can tell she's just pretending.

Mrs. O'Connell's face looks like she's about to throw up.

The school lawyer lady's eyes are still focused on that notepad. I wonder what she wrote on there.

Our lawyer--I guess he's not our lawyer anymore--is sweating like I'm sweating. I can feel my sweat, but I can see his, right around his collar.

Mrs. Kim's arm is moving a little. I can't see what she's doing under the table.

"Honey," Mom says in a small voice. "We should go. Josh has homework tonight, and we need to eat dinner."

Mrs. Kim's arm comes out from under the table, holding a phone. Her finger goes to touch the screen.

"WHAT ARE YOU DOING?" Dad explodes again.

Then, faster than I can see what's happening, the gun explodes, too. It's in Dad's hand, and Dad carries with one in the chamber. He always tells me that you must have one in the chamber because bad guys won't wait for you to load the mag. It sounds like someone slammed the door and the blinds slammed against the window. I usually have earplugs when we go shooting, so I didn't know what that's what it sounds like when it's really loud.

Mrs. Kim drops her phone. I think she's bleeding.

There's a long second when nobody moves.

Then, it starts.

Our lawyer and Dad jump up from their chairs about the same time. Dad takes out the mag that was on his belt, loads it, checks it's locked, and pulls the slide quickly. Our lawyer runs toward the door with his hand out to grab the handle.

He doesn't make it. Dad shoots again.

I've never seen anyone get shot before, not in real life. It's scary because one minute, they're talking about legal stuff, and then, the next minute, they're crying. Their arms fling out like rubber bands and they fall down. It doesn't look like on TV.

Miss Perry takes out her phone, so Dad shoots her, too. Her phone is purple with shiny fake diamonds on it. It flies up in the air.

Everyone who moves gets shot, and that is almost everyone.

Mr. Jones gets shot in the head.

The school lawyer lady gets shot in the chest, even though her notepad is in the way. There's a hole in her notepad.

Mrs. O'Connell gets shot in the face, and I don't even recognize her after the door slam sound.

Then it's just me and Mom and Dad and a room full of people who are dying. Dying is noisy. I hear someone gasping under the table.

Mom's puddle has grown into a lake. Her eyes don't look up from the lake on the table.

"What did you do?" she whispers.

"It's not my fault," Dad answers, and now his voice is shaking like Miss Perry's voice and the lawyer's voice did. "All they had to do was stay calm and give him what he needs."

"They *were*!" Mom wails. I've never heard Mom wail before, but I think that's what a wail sounds like. "They *were* calm. They *were* giving him what he needs."

"No, they weren't, or he'd be able to read! There's no way our kid is going to be able to survive out there-- he's stupid and he can't read. And you were *okay* with that? He should just be stupid and let everyone walk all over him? I shouldn't have left it to you because this crap happens. You tell him it's *okay* to be lazy? He must work harder! How's he going to catch up? You're an awful mother. He deserves better than you."

And then my Dad shoots my Mom in the back of the head.

My Dad killed my Mom and she's lying in a couple of globby pieces on the table in the conference room. Her face must be wet on the table from where her tears made that lake.

Our lawyer is blocking the door. I can still see part of his shiny, fancy tie peeking out from under his body. I think it's the tie--I don't think that's blood.

Mrs. Kim and the school lawyer lady disappeared --they must have fallen out of their chairs.

"You know I love you, right?" Dad says.

I guess it's not just moms and teachers who say nice things that aren't true.

"Yeah, I know, Dad," I say back because I have to say it back. "I love you, too."

"You know I'm a good person, and you know I had no choice."

"Yeah, I know."

"I just wanted them to teach you right. Make you better--you know?"

"Yeah, Dad. I know."

"But they didn't stay calm. And they weren't teaching you right. And I couldn't afford to send you private school. I thought about talking to your mom about homeschooling, but she's not a teacher. And that lawyer was charging $375 an hour. Can you believe that?"

I shake my head because I have to shake my head like I can't believe it, either.

"The police are going to come."

"Yeah, Dad."

"I can't go to jail. Then I'll never be able to get a job."

"Okay, Dad."

"And what'll happen to you when I'm gone?"

I understand what he's not saying. I can't read, but I understand a lot about what people don't say. Even if I couldn't, there are signs all over the room, and I'd have to be *really* stupid to miss them.

I think Mr. Jones was probably a great dad, if he had kids. I would have liked if he was my Dad. I don't think he would do what my Dad's not talking about doing.

"Dad?" I say as quietly as possible, so I don't piss him off. "I can still learn to read. I'll try harder. I heard Miss Perry tell Mrs. Ramirez they were going to be going to trainings to learn some more stuff to teach me. And I'm good at some other things. I'm pretty good at sports--football, you know. Remember when we used to throw the ball around? Remember? And I'm actually pretty good at music, too."

He looks at me like he feels sorry for me.

"You're okay at sports, but you'll never be able to do it professionally. You're not that good. You can't get a real job with music. And if you were going to learn to read, you had plenty of time to learn. You should have worked harder. You had time."

And when Dad says that is when I know for sure: I'm going to die because I'm stupid.

Agnes Bookbinder lives in the Pacific Northwest. She has been previously published in The Society of Classical Poets annual journal, the Worldwide Flash Fiction Competition, and The Southern Pacific Review.

moniker
pete donohue

he has been frightened of death as far back as he can remember. he hates his given name. can't even remember what it was now. so they call him moniker. the name of another name. it's a cruel humiliation. the boy with no real name. but he puts up with it. he has little choice. his identity drifts on the wind.

moniker begins life in a shitstorm. his father cuts his umbilical cord. with blooded rabbit teeth. & a tainted glaze in his eye. the way he has learnt to bite the bollocks off animals. in the frosted peat bogs of his native soil. where a move less cute than somebody else's can land you in turmoil. fuck you over forever. moniker's father pulls him away from that cruel countryside. moniker's father has other ideas. grand ideas.

one of an unlucky thirteen is moniker's father. the first brother dies before seeing the light of a third year. moniker never quite understands why. the elders explain it to him. in shelta. it makes no sense. even in his jesus mary & joseph mind. it makes no sense. this is a burden he will carry through life. as a heavy sack of freshly cut turves. dripping wet with the weight of the bogs. bending his supple back into a longbow that fires boomerang arrows. forever piercing his heart. fuel to cruelty.

moniker's father waits until spring. when the time comes to run. he knows to escape from the spade & the shovel. or else be cut down. bled dry. scooped up & slung into the fire. trapped in a life that seems worse than death. the stagnant slow burn. all ambitions up in smoke. no fate beyond embers. devoid of any catalytic spark. a future as potash. only to fertilise the next generation of small-minded bigots.

he flees to the next county. & the one after that. heading vaguely south. until he reaches the arsehole of the country. where bad blood & liquid diarrhea mingle around the torn rectum of a poisoned society. before leaking into the river. & out into the harbour. & onwards towards the atlantic. where sailors on the run hide from their past. & educate themselves & each other on the water. & when he has steeled himself with enough confidence. he takes off across the irish sea. into the next winter. with his damaged woman & his rebellious child moniker.

moniker grows from baby to boy. from boy to adolescent. from innocence into confusion. his father has swapped the spade & shovel for the pitch & sales patter. the money comes easy. there is free education. for moniker & his siblings. moniker becomes a teen of two nations. neither at ease with the other. there is nowhere for him to fit in. one nation rejects him as an émigré. the other as an immigrant. the turf cutter's blade has cleaved him down the middle. prised open his ribcage. severed his heart & soul. the suburbs feel cold. even in summertime.

from a vortex of uncertainty moniker witnesses every world he enters fall apart. there is violence in the home. there is ridicule in the school. there is bullying on the way between the two. there is refuge on darkening streets. but there is also danger. & there is the twilight excitement of temptation. the warm blanket of alcohol. the soft pillow of drugs. the rollercoaster of sexuality. the sweetest decline. he watches catholicism wank itself to death. escapes child buggery by the seat of his pants. begins burning black candles in celebration of the other. invents his own religion. which is every religion. & no religion. there is mental illness all around. both inside & out. it suffocates him.

when school's out for summer he begins to breathe again. moniker is fourteen. he feels more like twenty-four. sometimes thirty-four. he has done three years at secondary. bogtrotter makes good with the mind & gets free scholarship. to english public school. one of the most prestigious & expensive of this foreign landscape. in an alien world. he leaves behind the rough & tumble of the multi-racial working class. he considers it a prison sentence. no one has prepared him for the humiliation of being considered an oik amongst the elite. they wouldn't set him free for good behaviour. they didn't even expel him for bad behaviour. although many of his misfit mates have walked the plank to sink into better alternatives. anyhow. at least he has a teenage summer ahead of him.

august proves to be the hottest in moniker's memory. his ball-chewing poker-wielding belt-welting father is working away. his pill-popping crocodile-crying mother stays in bed each morning. only when the sun hits high noon does she drag herself up & out into the yard to bathe in the glory of it. along with that of her madness. the children fend for themselves. as they always have done. moniker's sister manages the younger ones. & moniker runs wild.

he spends his days on the hill of dreams. where all the miscreants alternatives creatives & rebels hang out. breakfasting on weed & special brew. skating danger paths on his slalom board. exploring the secret ancient tunnels that have witnessed almost every aspect of good & evil. dropping acid & fingering insane guitar chords. jamming with all those other dreaming hillbillies. helping to invent a new language that nobody would ever understand. unless they were there at the time. part of a unique cabal immortalised in time & space.

he spends his nights in the city backstreets & alleys. a world of sweaty neon & the constant threat & thrill of the unexpected. pornography prostitution gambling extortion money laundering intimidation violence amphetamine heroin cocaine. everything has an edge. & moniker walks them all with confidence. he feels like his whole life has been nothing but a practice run for this. he feels sharper than any edge. yet something is not quite right. moniker can't quite put his finger on it. maybe because it isn't yet there.

on the hottest day of the year moniker stands in front of his bedroom wardrobe mirror. it is early evening & the house is empty. his long hair is damp from the humidity. sweat glides down his cheeks & forehead. he gazes into his past & tries to imagine a future. his brain is scrambled by the disconnect. his guts burn in a swirl of emotional stew. in a momentary transcendence of mind & body he reaches into his soul. something needs to change & deep within he can feel what that is.

moniker takes scissors to his auburn hair. chops roughly at his curls as though doing penance for the sins of the world. when each tuft is as close to his scalp as he can get it he thinks of joan of arc. it is as if a great burden has been released. but it is still not enough. he needs to take it further. he moves to the bathroom & finds one of his father's razors. fills a jug with hot water. grabs an aerosol shaving foam. a flannel. a towel. takes them all back to his bedroom.

at the mirror he foams his scalp. wets the razor. & begins to scrape. starting at the front. doing his best with all the visible areas. but his inexperience soon draws blood. moniker doesn't care. he negotiates the back by feel alone. until at last he is satisfied. the newly bare skin stings. crimson rivulets run with his sweat. he cleans his head with the flannel. & towel dries. satisfied with the result. but this is still not enough.
moniker soaps his eyebrows. & soon they are gone. he thinks of syd barrett. of bowie. for the first time he notices his green eyes are almond shaped. it pleases him. he slips out of his clothes. soon not a single hair remains upon his body. he fetches his sister's make-up from her room. & paints himself a new face. he thinks of sinead o'connor. of britney spears. he raids his sister's clothes cupboard. bra & panties. summer frock. strappy sandals. they feel good to wear.

moniker admires herself in the mirror. she understands how she has begun a journey that will prove even harder than the one before. she doesn't mind. it all feels right. a sense of certainty at last. a sense of identity. of belonging. of hope. that cruel bastard should have bitten the balls off me as well as my cord she thinks. but she no longer fears him. he lies bleeding in his own private abode of the damned. clutching the handle of a zombie killer knife embedded in his stomach. minutes away from becoming a corpse. & only she knows.

this girl has reached a point in her life where she no longer fears death. she has some money. she has somewhere to go in the neon city. soon she will be fifteen. they'll never find her. & now she is comfortable with her name. now she is the monica she should always have been. the shitstorm has passed. her true-life story begins.

Pete Donohue works in community mental health in amazing Hastings on the Dirty South Coast of a proudly multi-cultural England and preserves his dubious sanity through creative writing, drawing, editing, reviewing and performing poetry, prose and music. He has published two poetry chapbooks to date (both sold out), with two more currently in production. His poetry, short stories and artwork have appeared in numerous underground and outlaw litzines, anthologies and digital literary vehicles, both in the US and UK. He is currently gathering up and adding to his short stories for a full published collection.

'moniker' first appeared in Glove Mag #6 (2018), a small limited edition uk litzine.

THE CASK OF AMONTILLADO
EDGAR ALLAN POE

The thousand injuries of Fortunato I had borne as I best could, but when he ventured upon insult, I vowed revenge. You, who so well know the nature of my soul, will not suppose, however, that I gave utterance to a threat. *At length* I would be avenged; this was a point definitely settled—but the very definitiveness with which it was resolved, precluded the idea of risk. I must not only punish but punish with impunity. A wrong is unredressed when retribution overtakes its redresser. It is equally unredressed when the avenger fails to make himself felt as such to him who has done the wrong.

It must be understood that neither by word nor deed had I given Fortunato cause to doubt my good will. I continued, as was my wont, to smile in his face, and he did not perceive that my smile *now* was at the thought of his immolation.

He had a weak point—this Fortunato—although in other regards he was a man to be respected and even feared. He prided himself on his connoisseurship in wine. Few Italians have the true virtuoso spirit. For the most part their enthusiasm is adopted to suit the time and opportunity—to practise imposture upon the British and Austrian *millionaires.* In painting and gemmary, Fortunato, like his countrymen, was a quack—but in the matter of old wines he was sincere. In this respect I did not differ from him materially: I was skillful in the Italian vintages myself and bought largely whenever I could.

It was about dusk, one evening during the supreme madness of the carnival season, that I encountered my friend. He accosted me with excessive warmth, for he had been drinking much. The man wore motley. He had on a tight-fitting parti-striped dress, and his head was surmounted by the conical cap and bells. I was so pleased to see him, that I thought I should never have done wringing his hand.

I said to him—"My dear Fortunato, you are luckily met. How remarkably well you are looking to-day! But I have received a pipe of what passes for Amontillado, and I have my doubts."

"How?" said he. "Amontillado? A pipe? Impossible! And in the middle of the carnival!"

"I have my doubts," I replied; "and I was silly enough to pay the full Amontillado price without consulting you in the matter. You were not to be found, and I was fearful of losing a bargain."

"Amontillado!"

"I have my doubts."

"Amontillado!"

"And I must satisfy them."

"Amontillado!"

"As you are engaged, I am on my way to Luchesi. If anyone has a critical turn, it is he. He will tell me—"

"Luchesi cannot tell Amontillado from Sherry."

"And yet some fools will have it that his taste is a match for your own."

"Come, let us go."

"Whither?"

"To your vaults."

"My friend, no; I will not impose upon your good nature. I perceive you have an engagement. Luchesi—"

"I have no engagement; —come."

"My friend, no. It is not the engagement, but the severe cold with which I perceive you are afflicted. The vaults are insufferably damp. They are encrusted with nitre."

"Let us go, nevertheless. The cold is merely nothing. Amontillado! You have been imposed upon. And as for Luchesi, he cannot distinguish Sherry from Amontillado."

Thus speaking, Fortunato possessed himself of my arm. Putting on a mask of black silk, and drawing a *roquelaire* closely about my person, I suffered him to hurry me to my palazzo.

There were no attendants at home; they had absconded to make merry in honour of the time. I had told them that I should not return until the morning and had given them explicit orders not to stir from the house. These orders were sufficient, I well knew, to ensure their immediate disappearance, one and all, as soon as my back was turned.

I took from their sconces two flambeaux, and giving one to Fortunato, bowed him through several suites of rooms to the archway that led into the vaults. I passed down a long and winding staircase, requesting him to be cautious as he followed. We came at length to the foot of the descent and stood together on the damp ground of the catacombs of the Montresors.

The gait of my friend was unsteady, and the bells upon his cap jingled as he strode.

"The pipe," said he.

"It is farther on," said I; "but observe the white web-work which gleams from these cavern walls."

He turned towards me and looked into my eyes with two filmy orbs that distilled the rheum of intoxication.

"Nitre?" he asked, at length.

"Nitre," I replied. "How long have you had that cough?"

"Ugh! ugh! ugh! —ugh! ugh! ugh! —ugh! ugh! ugh! —ugh! ugh! ugh! —ugh! ugh! ugh!"

My poor friend found it impossible to reply for many minutes.

"It is nothing," he said, at last.

"Come," I said, with decision, "we will go back; your health is precious. You are rich, respected, admired, beloved; you are happy, as once I was. You are a man to be missed. For me it is no matter. We will go back; you will be ill, and I cannot be responsible. Besides, there is Luchesi—"

"Enough," he said; "the cough is a mere nothing; it will not kill me. I shall not die of a cough."

"True—true," I replied; "and, indeed, I had no intention of alarming you unnecessarily—but you should use all proper caution. A draught of this Medoc will defend us from the damps."

Here I knocked off the neck of a bottle which I drew from a long row of its fellows that lay upon the mould.

"Drink," I said, presenting him the wine.

He raised it to his lips with a leer. He paused and nodded to me familiarly, while his bells jingled.

"I drink," he said, "to the buried that repose around us."

"And I to your long life."

He again took my arm, and we proceeded.

"These vaults," he said, "are extensive."

"The Montresors," I replied, "were a great and numerous family."

"I forget your arms."

"A huge human foot d'or, in a field azure; the foot crushes a serpent rampant whose fangs are imbedded in the heel."

"And the motto?"

"*Nemo me impune lacessit.*"

"Good!" he said.

The wine sparkled in his eyes and the bells jingled. My own fancy grew warm with the Medoc. We had passed through walls of piled bones, with casks and puncheons intermingling, into the inmost recesses of catacombs. I paused again, and this time I made bold to seize Fortunato by an arm above the elbow.

"The nitre!" I said; "see, it increases. It hangs like moss upon the vaults. We are below the river's bed. The drops of moisture trickle among the bones. Come, we will go back ere it is too late. Your cough—"

"It is nothing," he said; "let us go on. But first, another draught of the Medoc."

I broke and reached him a flagon of De Grave. He emptied it at a breath. His eyes flashed with a fierce light. He laughed and threw the bottle upwards with a gesticulation I did not understand.

I looked at him in surprise. He repeated the movement—a grotesque one.

"You do not comprehend?" he said.

"Not I," I replied.

"Then you are not of the brotherhood."

"How?"

"You are not of the masons."

"Yes, yes," I said; "yes, yes."

"You? Impossible! A mason?"

"A mason," I replied.

"A sign," he said, "a sign."

"It is this," I answered, producing a trowel from beneath the folds of my *roquelaire*.

"You jest," he exclaimed, recoiling a few paces. "But let us proceed to the Amontillado."

"Be it so," I said, replacing the tool beneath the cloak and again offering him my arm. He leaned upon it heavily. We continued our route in search of the Amontillado. We passed through a range of low arches, descended, passed on, and descending again, arrived at a deep crypt, in which the foulness of the air caused our flambeaux rather to glow than flame.

At the most remote end of the crypt there appeared another less spacious. Its walls had been lined with human remains, piled to the vault overhead, in the fashion of the great catacombs of Paris. Three sides of this interior crypt were still ornamented in this manner. From the fourth side the bones had been thrown down, and lay promiscuously upon the earth, forming at one point a mound of some size. Within the wall thus exposed by the displacing of the bones, we perceived a still interior recess, in depth about four feet in width three, in height six or seven. It seemed to have been constructed for no especial use within itself but formed merely the interval between two of the colossal supports of the roof of the catacombs and was backed by one of their circumscribing walls of solid granite.

It was in vain that Fortunato, uplifting his dull torch, endeavoured to pry into the depth of the recess. Its termination the feeble light did not enable us to see.

"Proceed," I said; "herein is the Amontillado. As for Luchesi—"

"He is an ignoramus," interrupted my friend, as he stepped unsteadily forward, while I followed immediately at his heels. In an instant he had reached the extremity of the niche, and finding his progress arrested by the rock, stood stupidly bewildered. A moment more and I had fettered him to the granite. In its surface were two iron staples, distant from each other about two feet, horizontally. From one of these depended a short chain, from the other a padlock. Throwing the links about his waist, it was but the work of a few seconds to secure it. He was too much astounded to resist. Withdrawing the key I stepped back from the recess.

"Pass your hand," I said, "over the wall; you cannot help feeling the nitre. Indeed, it is *very* damp. Once more let me *implore* you to return. No? Then I must positively leave you. But I must first render you all the little attentions in my power."

"The Amontillado!" ejaculated my friend, not yet recovered from his astonishment.

"True," I replied; "the Amontillado."

As I said these words, I busied myself among the pile of bones of which I have before spoken. Throwing them aside, I soon uncovered a quantity of building stone and mortar. With these materials and with the aid of my trowel, I began vigorously to wall up the entrance of the niche.

I had scarcely laid the first tier of the masonry when I discovered that the intoxication of Fortunato had in a great measure worn off. The earliest indication I had of this was a low moaning cry from the depth of the recess. It was *not* the cry of a drunken man. There was then a long and obstinate silence. I laid the second tier, and the third, and the fourth; and then I heard the furious vibrations of the chain. The noise lasted for several minutes, during which, that I might hearken to it with the more satisfaction, I ceased my labours and sat down upon the bones. When at last the clanking subsided, I resumed the trowel, and finished without interruption the fifth, the sixth, and the seventh tier. The wall was now nearly upon a level with my breast. I again paused, and holding the flambeaux over the mason-work, threw a few feeble rays upon the figure within.

A succession of loud and shrill screams, bursting suddenly from the throat of the chained form, seemed to thrust me violently back. For a brief moment I hesitated—I trembled. Unsheathing my rapier, I began to grope with it about the recess; but the thought of an instant reassured me. I placed my hand upon the solid fabric of the catacombs and felt satisfied. I reapproached the wall; I replied to the yells of him who clamoured. I re-echoed—I aided—I surpassed them in volume and in strength. I did this, and the clamourer grew still.

It was now midnight, and my task was drawing to a close. I had completed the eighth, the ninth, and the tenth tier. I had finished a portion of the last and the eleventh; there remained but a single stone to be fitted and plastered in. I struggled with its weight; I placed it partially in its destined position. But now there came from out the niche a low laugh that erected the hairs upon my head. It was succeeded by a sad voice, which I had difficulty in recognizing as that of the noble Fortunato. The voice said—

"Ha! ha! ha! —he! he! he! —a very good joke indeed—an excellent jest. We shall have many a rich laugh about it at the palazzo—he! he! he! —over our wine—he! he! he!"

"The Amontillado!" I said.

"He! he! he! —he! he! he! —yes, the Amontillado. But is it not getting late? Will not they be awaiting us at the palazzo, the Lady Fortunato and the rest? Let us be gone."

"Yes," I said, "let us be gone."

"For the love of God, Montresor!"

"Yes," I said, "for the love of God!"

But to these words I hearkened in vain for a reply. I grew impatient. I called aloud—

"Fortunato!"

No answer. I called again—

"Fortunato—"

No answer still. I thrust a torch through the remaining aperture and let it fall within. There came forth in reply only a jingling of the bells. My heart grew sick on account of the dampness of the catacombs. I hastened to make an end of my labour. I forced the last stone into its position; I plastered it up. Against the new masonry I re-erected the old rampart of bones. For the half of a century no mortal has disturbed them. *In pace requiescat!*

BEFORE THE LAW
FRANZ KAFKA

Before the law sits a gatekeeper. To this gatekeeper comes a man from the country who asks to gain entry into the law. But the gatekeeper says that he cannot grant him entry at the moment. The man thinks about it and then asks if he will be allowed to come in later on.

"It is possible," says the gatekeeper, "But not now."

At the moment the gate to the law stands open as always, and the gatekeeper walks to the side, so the man bends over in order to see through the gate into the inside.

When the gatekeeper notices that, he laughs and says: "if it tempts you so much, try it in spite of my prohibition. But take note: I am powerful. And I am only the most lowly gatekeeper. But from room to room stand gatekeepers, each more powerful than the other. I can't endure even one glimpse of the third."

The man from the country had not expected such difficulties: the law should always be accessible for everyone, he thinks, but as he now looks more closely at the gatekeeper in his fur coat, at his large pointed nose and his long, thin Tartar's beard, he decides it would be better to wait until he gets permission to go inside.

The gatekeeper gives him a stool and allows him to sit down at the side in front of the gate. There he sits for days and years. He makes many attempts to be let in, and he wears the gatekeeper out with his requests.

The gatekeeper often interrogates him briefly, questioning him about his homeland and many other things, but they are indifferent questions, the kind great men put, and at the end he always tells him once more that he cannot let him inside yet.

The man, who has equipped himself with many things for his journey, spends everything, no matter how valuable, to win over the gatekeeper. The latter takes it all, but as he does so, says, "I am taking this only so that you do not think you have failed to do anything."

During the many years the man observes the gatekeeper almost continuously. He forgets the other gatekeepers, and this one seems to him the only obstacle for entry into the law. He curses the unlucky circumstance, in the first years thoughtlessly and out loud, later, as he grows old, he still mumbles to himself.

He becomes childish and, since in the long years studying the gatekeeper, he has come to know the fleas of his fur collar, he even asks the fleas to help him persuade the gatekeeper.

Finally, his eyesight grows weak, and he does not know whether things are really darker around him or whether his eyes are merely deceiving him. But he recognizes now in the darkness an illumination which breaks inextinguishably out of the gateway to the law. Now he no longer has much time to live. Before his death he gathers in his head all his experiences of the entire time up into the one question which he has not yet put to the gatekeeper. He waves to him, since he can no longer lift up his stiffening body.

The gatekeeper has to bend way down to him, for the great difference has changed things to the disadvantage of the man.

"What do you still want to know, then?" asks the gatekeeper. "You are insatiable."

"Everyone strives after the law, says the man, "so how is it that in these many years no one except me has requested entry.

The gatekeeper sees that the man is already dying and, in order to reach his diminishing sense of hearing, he shouts at him. "Here no one else can gain entry, since this entrance was assigned only to you. I'm going to close it."

THE TERRORIST
Stephen Moran

Scott walked south along Central Street, passing familiar houses that never seemed to change, get painted, or age with the years. He stopped at the corner of Quaker Street and debated taking the long way home. He decided against it and continued along Central. Dried, dead leaves and the remains of a snowstorm crunched underfoot as he made his way up the hill before taking a right onto Providence Street.

Quickening his pace when home came into view, he avoided looking at the graveyard across the street. Bounding up the small slope of the front yard, he jumped the wall onto the driveway and opened the cellar door.

The kennels stood on the left. Food spilled over the bowls, and the water contained dust and dirt, a foul smell filling the area. Tracing a hand over the top of the first cage, his fingers came away covered in dust. He made for the stairs and climbed them slowly. The faded, wooden steps creaked, and a coffee can filled with rusted nails shook as he approached the door.

He pushed the door open until it thudded against the wall. In the living room, boxes and trash filled the space. A lone mattress without bedding occupied the center of the room. Next to the bed, there was an ashtray overflowing with crushed cigarettes. A television rested on the floor. He glanced into the kitchen, but it was empty. He stopped at the first room on the left. A *Transformers* poster hung at an odd angle by a single tack, and broken Tonka trucks littered the floor. Scott closed the door, pressing his forehead again the wood.

He continued down the hall and came to the door. The last door on the left was his room. Turning the knob, he pushed the door open. There was a writing desk piled with papers and books against the far wall. Otherwise, the room was empty. He sat in the desk chair. Reaching under the monitor, he pressed the button and waited for the screen to come to life.

Clicking the mouse, he opened a file. He cracked his knuckles and placed his fingers on the keyboard.

"I believe in dragons.'"

A crashing sound woke Scott from his sleep. He opened his eyes to see the roof ripped from the house and a great, coal-black dragon towering above the ruins. The dragon seized him, with massive talons digging into his shoulders, and rose into the sky. The wind stung Scott's face while the dragon carried him with great speed over the surrounding towns.

"Slow down," Scott said to the dragon.

"As you wish," the dragon answered, coming to a stop mid-air before hurtling toward the ground. The moment before impact, the dragon veered and flew over the next hill. Landing in a wide clearing, the dragon deposited Scott on the ground and took a position next to a great oak tree.

"What do you want?" Scott asked, taking several steps away from the dragon.

"What do you want is more like. And why bother running? If I wanted to kill you, you wouldn't be alive."

Scott shook his head and rubbed at his eyes. "Is this a dream?"

The dragon breathed fire at him, and Scott dove for cover. "Perhaps that will wake you."

"I'm awake. Now, tell me why you destroyed my house," Scott asked, standing once again.

"An accident. My apologies. I came into existence from your belief, and I am yours to command."

Taking a few steps toward the dragon, Scott ran a hand through his hair before taking a pack of cigarettes from his pocket. "You'll do anything I want?" Scott asked.

The dragon laughed and snorted smoke, "I have no moral clause."

Scott paced for a few minutes, smoking and pulling at his beard. He smoked the entire cigarette before he spoke again. "Burn Town Hall," he ordered.

The dragon laughed again and lowered a shoulder to allow Scott to climb on his back. Once Scott settled into position, the dragon launched them skyward, heading with much haste toward Main Street. Soon, Town Hall came into view. Scott noticed no movement or other signs of life in the parking lot or windows.

"Hold on," the dragon said as the building came into range.

Scott attempted to speak, but the dragon spit fire, bathing Town Hall in light. He held on as the assault continued, and the dragon hovered in the air to fire again and again on the defenseless building. Flames engulfed the second story within minutes. Scott smiled with satisfaction as the sirens began to wail.

"Burn it all!" Scott screamed in the air.

The dragon spun and sprayed fire in all directions, igniting the surrounding houses. The dragon put fire to every house in town.

The growing chorus of sirens followed the fiery show. Scott heard a gunshot. The dragon snatched the man who fired from the ground, snapping him in half.

As the dragon lifted Scott from the flaming wreckage of Town Hall, he realized he had been shot.

Scott's hand found the wound near his temple and clamped against the gushing blood. The dragon swooped toward the next target. Scott slipped and plummeted toward the ground. As he fell, blood streamed into the air from the wound.

"Peace," Scott said a moment before he crashed.

Chief of Police John Brown waited on the front steps, looking around in every direction. He stopped to make a small nod of greeting to each man and woman on the task force. Pressing a finger against his lips, Chief Brown placed a boot on the first of four concrete steps leading to the one-story ranch. A gunshot shattered the silence.

SWAT swarmed ahead of him and entered the house. He listened to their calls as they cleared each room. He followed down the hall to the master bedroom. Walking inside, he saw Scott's body at the desk, dead with a gunshot wound to the temple. The gun rested under the chair, a spent casing beside it.

"Damn it, we won't get to question him. Search the place," he said, taking a pipe from his pocket. With a deft hand, he packed the bowl and lit it.

He observed the scene but didn't interrupt. Chief Brown placed a callused index finger on an engraving along the handle of the pipe: *DH*. The initials of his grandfather, a policeman long ago. Had he ever encountered such a scene in this small town?

Two EMTs entered the room, arms loaded with medical bags and cases.

"It's a suicide," a detective commented. The EMTs checked for signs of life despite the pronouncement.

"What can you expect from a Holden?" Chief Brown said. "What can you expect from a coward who threw a firebomb into town Hall?" He puffed at the pipe and watched the medic examine the body.

The young man glanced up at the chief. "How many died in the Town Hall explosion?"

"Four. Two officers, a dispatcher, and a janitor, that poor bastard. He wasn't even scheduled to work. Was just there picking up his paycheck." John puffed again on the pipe.

"How can you remain calm?" the medic asked.

"I don't know, you just do, or you lose your composure. It's not easy on days like today. That business at the Town Hall is the worst I've ever seen."

He wanted to say more, to speak about his grandfather and tradition and doing the job without letting emotion get the best of you, say *I've seen a few cops die. That's part of the job, kid,* but a commotion from the hallway interrupted him. Chief Brown followed the din of voices from the basement. He took the stairs down two at a time, careful not to hit his head against the low wall over the landing.

The sea of cops parted to reveal a massive hole in the concrete foundation. Flashlights illuminated a tunnel. Chief Brown grabbed a lantern from a patrolman and plunged into the opening.

He entered a small room shaped like a hobbit hole. Thrusting the lantern forward revealed three skeletons, one adult and two children, seated at a small table, arranged as if at a tea party. John panned the lantern around the small space, light touching bones and remains buried into the wall, cemented in time. Skeletons ringed the family seated at tea, eternal witnesses to the party.

His mouth fell open, and the pipe dropped to the dirt floor. Struggling to breathe, Chief Brown wanted to tear his eyes from the skeletons at tea-time, but he felt frozen to the ground. One of the children's hands reached towards a tiny cup on the table. The sparkling porcelain hovered out of the child's reach. How odd to see a clean cup in a room of filth and dust! He heard words in his mind, and they made him wretch. *He spent time in this room. He was having tea with the skeletons ...*

He clutched at the wall for support to keep from falling. Without making a sign that he noticed the loss of his favorite pipe, Chief Brown retraced his steps to the front door and left the house. Staggering down the slope of the front yard, he pulled the badge from his chest and tossed it on the ground. He didn't get into his service vehicle, but instead continued along Providence Street, ignoring the yells and screams of cops running after him, trying to make him stop.

BOOK OF BIRDS by L. M. Bryski – A coming of age mystery set in post WWII Canada. Find out why readers say there's something special about *Book of Birds*.

BLOOD CHILL by L. M. Bryski – Blood Chill is a fast-paced medical thriller set in a post-apocalyptic Canadian winter.

LOVE AND QUARTERS by Gabriel Ricard – The world is a badly run 1890's-style asylum, but at least there's a lot of good stuff on TV. A poetry collection with uncanny commentary on current day America.

BONDAGE NIGHT by Gabriel Ricard – A savage, unreasonable love story for savage, unreasonable times. *Bondage Night* dares tell the whole sordid truth about happily ever after. This love story for modern times pulls no punches and depicts an affair between two broken, hopelessly mismatched people and the inevitable destruction as they try to stay together.

CLOUDY DAYS, STILL NIGHTS by Austin Davis – The debut poetry collection by Austin Davis, *Cloudy Days, Still Nights* is an earnest exploration of love that steers clear of sentimentality.

SECOND CIVIL WAR by Austin Davis – A call to action for his generation, *Second Civil War* implores the youth to stand against bigotry and to vote!

CRUMBLING UTOPIAN PIPEDREAM by Scott Wozniak – A book of poetry born of the streets. "No book I've read fucks around less than *Crumbling Utopian Pipedream* by Scott Wozniak. You want a blurb, there's your blurb." Review by Anthony Dragonetti.

ELLA by Stephen Moran – A coming of age psychological thriller about a young woman's cross-country journey of discovery, revenge, and murder. It's a romance about a woman and the men she chops into small pieces. WARNING for graphic violence.

SERVER by Stephen Moran – A novella told in short story chapters; *Server* is unlike any book you've ever read. Part manifesto, part fiction, it catalogs the decent of Scott Holden into madness.

THE TERRORIST OF PROVIDENCE STREET by Stephen Moran – Nothing is as it seems. The original edition of *SERVER*, a novella told in short story chapters, with an ending that's both shocking and illuminating.

STORMING JERICHO by Shelby Kent-Stewart – A fast-paced romance thriller that will put spice in your reading list. A perfect book for an evening by the fire.

THE MOURNING AFTER by Charles Bivona – A memoir painted in poetry and essays, *The Mourning After* traces the fractured narrative of the writer's life. From his childhood in the aftermath of the Vietnam War, to his academic years in the shadow of 9/11, the portrait that emerges from this arresting collection is one of devastating loss, deep love, and a unique introspection on what it means to be an American.

MEMOIRS IN FRAGMENTS by Charles Bivona – Twenty poems on love and trauma spanning ten years of the poet's life.

48586741R00085

Printed in Poland
by Amazon Fulfillment
Poland Sp. z o.o., Wrocław